I0574036

MIDNIGHT CARESS

LISA MARIE RICE

OLIVERHEBERBOOKS

All rights reserved.

No part of this publication may be sold, copied, distributed, reproduced or transmitted in any form or by any means, mechanical or digital, including photocopying and recording or by any information storage and retrieval system without the prior written permission of both the publisher, Oliver Heber Books and the author, Lisa Marie Rice, except in the case of brief quotations embodied in critical articles and reviews.

PUBLISHER'S NOTE: This is a work of fiction. Names, characters, places, and incidents either are the product of the author's imagination or are used fictitiously. Any resemblance to actual persons, living or dead, business establishments, events, or locales is entirely coincidental.

Published by Oliver-Heber Books

Midnight Embrace © by Lisa Marie Rice

Cover Design by Sweet 'N Spicy Designs

0 9 8 7 6 5 4 3 2 1

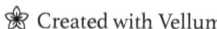 Created with Vellum

1

NATIONAL SURVEILLANCE OFFICE, CHANTILLY, VIRGINIA

"Well, fuck," her boss, Henry Yu said.

Riley Robinson was a little shocked. She'd never heard Henry swear. Her boss was tall, elegant, well-spoken. The epitome of cool. He wasn't cool now. He looked like he'd been run over by a truck. Twice.

They were in her office. She'd recently been promoted, so she had an office to herself—not much larger than a broom closet, but hers. You came in on invitation or because you were higher in the pecking order. Henry was here because she'd asked him to come, even though he was, of course, higher in the pecking order, too.

He looked down at the image from equatorial Congo that was frozen on her tablet. The tablet that was, at that moment, unconnected to the NSO network. It showed, with astonishing clarity, men in black combat uniforms with a flame outlined in gold on the sleeves. The universally recognized symbol of a security company called The Sommers Group. Effective, ruthless and brutal.

They were attacking a group of civilians, camped out in the jungle. A little tent city of scientists, a couple of work stations set up on card tables. They were in a clearing that had been hacked out of the jungle, dead branches lying on the ground.

The soldiers came out of the jungle as one, in a coordinated attack. There were ten of them, moving in synchrony, as if rehearsed. In a circle, stationed about three meters apart.

There was no sound in the video, of course. It was being recorded from twenty-five thousand miles up in the sky.

The soldiers appeared out of the jungle and the scientists lifted their heads, one by one. One of the soldiers shouted an order. You could see his mouth open wide, the tendons in his neck standing out. One scientist in a white lab coat shook his head, *no*. An instant later, the back of his head blew out. You couldn't see the bullet going in but you could see bone and brains blowing out the back.

He crumpled instantly to the ground, a pale pink mist lingering in the air where his head had been.

The soldiers had placed big black duffel bags on the ground. The order had apparently been to fill the bags with the scientific equipment. The scientists began to work but apparently not quickly enough. A scientist wearing shorts under a lab coat was meticulous. One of the soldiers grew impatient as beakers were carefully and slowly placed in a big plastic container, and he used his rifle butt to bash in the scientist's head. The scientist crumpled to the ground, blood pooling around his head.

There was something wrong with the soldiers. Some were shaking, they all seemed to be super excited, barely in control of themselves, shifting from foot to foot. One happened to look up and Riley stepped back at the expression on his face. Crazed. Lips drawn back from his teeth, jaws rippling with tension.

The satellite image of the attack was closing, the earth's rotation moving the area away from the non-geosynchronous satellite. The final image in the upper corner was of half the soldiers disappearing back into the jungle, carrying now-heavy-looking duffel bags, and the other half mowing down the scientists, leaving dead bodies and smoke.

The satellite moved on, showing green jungle canopy, dark, endless.

Riley drew a big breath. "That's what our program captured. But this is what will go on the news in a few minutes, for the second or third time. You might not have seen it yet, but you've heard about it."

Henry nodded and watched carefully as she showed another video. The same one, except that the soldiers weren't Sommers Group mercenaries. They wore Chinese uniforms. Riley had looked over sat photos of Chinese military bases for over a year and recognized the uniforms of the People's Liberation Army. They were wearing field uniforms number 07, improbably uncrumpled, which would mean they hadn't marched to the scientific camp but presumably had deployed from nearby. The Congo jungle in June was merciless.

There were two captains, with the three-stars-on-a-bar collar insignia. The others were foot soldiers. They all had that crazed, hopped-up look the Sommers Group soldiers had had. Except these were Chinese soldiers, notorious for their discipline and rigor. Thousands of hours studying photos and videos of Chinese soldiers in military camps, and Riley had never seen any Chinese soldier behave in an undisciplined way. Not once.

"The video has been GANned," Henry said, and Riley nodded. It had been subjected to a Generative Adversarial Network process.

Deepfaked.

The Chinese soldiers were a deepfake. An excellent one.

"What are we going to do?" Riley whispered. It was like holding a powerful grenade in your hand and someone had pulled the pin. Something really bad was about to happen, and soon.

Henry shrugged. Riley was fond of him. He was a good boss and knew his stuff, but he wasn't decisive.

"Henry—we might be going to *war* over this. Over a lie."

His face tightened. "I know."

What started as a trickle of news was now starting to be a flood, a tsunami, taking up three-quarters of news programs. An exponential progression.

"Henry, we have to take this to someone."

"I know," he repeated.

Damn. Was he going to stand there like a dummy and repeat *I know?*

"Who do we go to? The Pentagon? The White House? Congress?"

He shook his head, as if trying to shake himself awake. "Not Congress."

No, not Congress. "We have to find someone to listen to us. Everyone is on super alert and nervous. On one podcast I heard that the whole military is going to Defcon 4 and Defcon 3 isn't far behind." Which was super scary shit. Defcon 3, known as Round House, was an increase in force readiness. Defcon 2, known as Fast Pace, meant armed forces were ready to deploy and engage in less than six hours.

And of course, it could all go to Defcon 1, known as Cocked Pistol, which was nuclear war.

"I'm going to contact my boss, Morris Sartan, first. Then I know someone at Homeland Security. He's a reasonable man. Let me see if I can get in touch with him."

"Here." Riley placed a flash drive in his hand. "That's what I just showed you. It's encrypted." She wrote a long string of letters and numbers on a piece of notepaper and tore it. "I want to say *swallow this*, but of course it would be useless. It's the code to decrypt it. Fold it tightly and put it somewhere on your person where a guard wouldn't find it if you were frisked."

Henry took the strip of paper, folded it into a tight cube and put it in his suit jacket pocket. His hands trembled. "I'll think of something better, while on my way over. I'll get in touch as soon as I've spoken to the boss and then my friend, okay?"

Riley nodded. "I think I might go home early. But I'll always answer my cell. I'm too agitated to stay here."

Henry nodded. He opened his mouth, shut it, and left. Riley understood. There wasn't much to say. Either she was wrong, and was risking her career, Henry's career, and possibly jail, or she was right and the risk was nuclear warfare and the annihilation of civilization over a scam.

God, she hoped she was wrong. She had serious skills. If she lost her job here, she could always find another one. As a matter of fact, her friends Felicity, Hope and Emma were always on her case to come to Portland, Oregon and work for their company, Alpha Security International. A good company, they said. Where they had maximum freedom, a great salary, and worked with good guys.

No hierarchy. No office politics.

The NSO was okay, the work was interesting, but it was a massive bureaucracy, and she was a cog in a huge mechanism.

The way her friends described their bosses, there would be no problem talking to them, putting this whole mess in their capable hands.

Right now, at NSO, she had nowhere to go. She'd never met the new Big Boss, who'd just arrived two weeks before. She had no idea what to do, whom to approach. Her immediate boss, Henry, obviously didn't trust people higher up the pecking order, if he wanted to avoid everyone in-house. He was going to take this to his boss, Morris Sartan, but he didn't sound enthusiastic.

Riley trusted her friends in Portland more than she trusted

anyone at work. And she had a secret way of getting in touch with them.

The HER room. A place in the dark web only they had access to. They used it to ask for help, like a bat signal. She was about to call them when she saved her life by looking up.

She had a room of her own, a tiny glass-enclosed cubicle. The vertical blinds were half open, which allowed her to keep an eye on what was happening in the big room outside, but which blocked a view of her office from outside.

Three people entered the big room at the far end. Three men, tall, fit, in military uniform though she didn't recognize what branch they served in. They were athletic, wore hard scowls, and were armed.

They were definitely not in-house security. She'd never seen them before. And then one of the men turned to the side to ask a question of a female colleague. She paused, turned, and pointed. Straight at Riley's office.

As the man turned, she stiffened with terror. The man had a flame outlined in gold stitched on the arm of his jacket. The symbol of the Sommers Group.

The mercenaries of the Sommers group.

Here.

Coming for her.

Her heart was pounding so hard it felt like her chest vibrated. She was used to making inferences with insufficient data, but this data wasn't insufficient at all. She'd uncovered criminal behavior by members of the Sommers group and, *surprise surprise*, here they were. After her.

The three men were walking—almost marching—in synch toward her office. She had about half a minute to disappear.

But her office was glass-enclosed, the windows to the outside were welded in place, because God forbid NSO employees get whiffs of fresh air. Which suited them, nerds all. Fresh air was poison to nerds.

She was on the fourth floor, so even if she managed to break the glass, which was bullet-resistant, she couldn't escape, she'd just splat on the ground. The façade of the building was smooth, not even a ledge to inch across.

But... she shared an internal door with Sylvie Carter, an IR analyst who was back in California dealing with a sick mom. They were friends and had long ago unlocked the door between them.

Riley had the key on her fob, because she'd forgotten to take it off. In an instant, she had the door open, shot through to Sylvie's office and locked the door behind her. She looked around. The only place to hide was Sylvie's bathroom, on the opposite wall. No choice.

She was closing the bathroom door behind her when she heard noises coming from her office. It only took them a second to realize her office was empty. Angry male voices. Someone rattled the door between her office and Sylvie's, but stopped when it was clear that the door was locked.

"Check the video feeds," she heard one man say and her heart sank.

There wasn't a video feed in her office, but there were cams all along the corridors. How was she going to get out if they were following the feeds throughout the building?

The three exited her room. Riley cracked open the bathroom door and looked through the window into the corridor. Like her, Sylvie kept the blinds just so—you could look out but not look in. The operatives marched almost in lockstep past Sylvie's office. One, two, three. No one left behind in her office. They were marching to where they thought she might be. Where was that? Riley rarely left her office except to grab a coffee in the rec room down the hall, or to consult with colleagues. She didn't like wasting time at work.

Still, they were looking for her and presumably weren't going to stop.

Oh God, she needed to get out of the building without them knowing! But where could she go? How to find a place those thugs couldn't follow her?

She had to get out of Dodge, and she couldn't do it alone.

Thank God she had her cell. She sat down behind the desk, on the floor, and pulled up her Secret Sauce, an independent wifi that bypassed the building's servers and turned her cell into a sat phone. The brass would have said that it was impossible. Personal cell phones were blocked inside the building, springing to life the instant you crossed Lee Road.

But she was able to call the HER Room, a place on the darkweb accessible only to Felicity O'Brien, Hope Ellis, Emma Holland and her, Riley. They'd all worked together at the NSA and had had the Boss from Hell, and had set up the HER room to warn each other when he was on the prowl. And it had served as a Bat Signal for when one of them got in trouble.

Hope had used it, Emma had used it, and now it was her turn. She needed her buddies.

Riley logged in to the secret site that no one would ever find except for her best buddies. Her best buddies who also worked at a security company made up of really tough good guys.

If there was ever a moment she needed help from tough good guys, now was it. She plugged in an earbud because the call sign was the King of the Goblins in all his nasty, blubbery glory screaming *Bring up the Bonebreaker!* It was loud.

Rising, she went to the door and peeked out. There were fifteen people in cubicles. Cubicles in the NSO were high. Riley could only see the tops of the heads of the tallest people. And they weren't sitting straight up, they were hunched over their keyboards like everyone did.

No one paid her the slightest bit of attention.

But there were some bass tones in the distance. Coming from the left, from the administrative offices. Nobody on the floor had a bass voice. There were ten men on her floor, and barely enough testosterone to supply a hummingbird.

Riley eased out of Sophie's office door, trying hard to look around her without looking insane. The bass tones were coming closer. They'd checked the offices in that wing and would move through her area on to Acquisitions and then to Contracts.

She walked as fast as she could, without running, towards the Contracts offices. Most of the Contracts department was at the CIA for a briefing. With any luck, it would be deserted.

She was so tempted to call Henry, but he might be at a delicate moment, telling someone in the hierarchy that the US might be planning on going to war over a mistake. A deepfake.

Slipping into the Contracts corridor, the background noise level sank. It had that unmistakable feel of an abandoned area. All the Contracts people were staying at a small hotel in Langley while the week-long briefing was going on.

Slumped against a wall, she brought up a site on the dark web and was about to log in when she heard a commotion back in the bull pen. She didn't dare walk out into the open in case the Sommer Group operatives were still out there. But there was a workaround. The security cameras in public spaces were on a separate network. It would have taken some time to hack into a specific office, but it was relatively easy to hack into the public spaces videocams. She chose the camera on the wall her office shared because it felt like the voices came from that side of the bullpen.

Sure enough, there was a knot of office workers congregated around a person who held his cellphone so everyone could see the image on the screen. Billy Parsons, a new hire. Smart, with abysmal social skills. She couldn't quite see his cellphone screen, but those who could were showing shock. Two covered their mouths.

Then, one by one, their cellphones must have pinged, and they all pulled out their own cells. She'd set hers to vibrate and opened it. Riley gasped.

They showed Henry, on the floor, with half his face blown off. A couple of images showed Henry's entire body, unmistakably lifeless, sprawled on the floor.

Then her screen showed an image taken from a news blog she was familiar with, with odious politics. The writers seemed to be plugged into politics and they were always the first to publish.

She logged onto the site and there it was. Poor Henry's body, taking up most of the home page. Above it, in screaming red capital letters: CHINESE NATIONAL GUILTY OF SPYING.

She almost couldn't breathe. Henry was not a Chinese national, he was American-born, third generation, a descendent of Chinese grandparents who had escaped Mao's Cultural Revolution in the late 60s. And... guilty of *spying?* What the hell? The NSO was a thinly disguised spy agency. Of course... and then her heart dropped.

That wasn't what the website meant. They meant spying for *China.* Anyone who knew Henry would realize how absurd that was, but anyone who didn't know him. . .

She switched back to the video cameras of the bullpen.

Oh God.

At the edges of the video camera, she caught one of the Sommers Group operatives, walking back to her office, opening the door and peering inside again. Thinking she might have returned to her office.

If they could kill Henry, they could definitely kill her. And would. It was her algo that had uncovered the deep fake.

She stood up and ran to the end of the corridor, finishing entering the password for the HER room on the run.

The Goblin King made his appearance as she ran. She nearly sobbed when Emma Holland's face appeared. "Emma, I need help!" she whisper-screamed.

Emma would help. She and Hope and Felicity—Riley could count on them for anything. Riley didn't have the bandwidth, or the time, or her laptop, to map out an exit on the run. Her friends in Portland, who worked for one of the top security firms in the world, would help.

But then Emma's face shrank to half the screen and another one appeared. A man, leaning on his fists, face close to the camera. A very handsome face. Blue-black hair, dark blue eyes. Clean, sharp features.

"Riley, I'm Pierce, a colleague." Her friends worked at a security company that was the opposite of the Sommers Group. "And I'm in DC. How can I help?"

Riley had to suppress a cry of relief. Hope, Emma and Felicity would do everything possible to help her but they were across the country. And they were smart but not operators. Hope once described the men she worked with as super nice... to them. But dangerous to the bad guys.

The Sommers Group was as bad as they come.

To help, Pierce had to know the situation. It was hard to sum up, while she felt the drumbeat of terror pounding through her. "You know the tensions between us and China?"

He frowned, dark eyebrows meeting over his sharp blade of a nose. "Yeah. Bad news."

"The worst. But it's a lie. It's based on a lie and I have the proof. Chinese soldiers did not attack US scientists. But the people after me don't want that to come out. They are the

Sommers Group and they are the attackers." She put up a photo, where the Sommers Group logo could be clearly seen on the mercenaries' sleeves. Dead scientists on the ground, out of control PMCs baying at the sky. Riley could hear Emma and Hope sucking in a breath. "They killed my boss."

Moisture on her cheeks. She swiped angrily at her face. "And now they are after me."

Pierce was listening but he was also consulting Hope and Emma. "Okay. I'm about twenty minutes out. Can you hide for twenty minutes? Hope and Emma are going to wipe out the NSO's security cam system."

If there were no cams... "Yeah, I think so."

He cocked his head, listening to someone off screen. "Emma says to go to the sub-basement and hide there. Did you make the changes to your cell?"

Meaning—did she turn her cell into a satphone? That could operate independently of cell towers that had been turned off.

"Yeah."

"Right. Hold on. We're mapping out... okay. I'll send you a text when it's time to come up. Emma says to come up in Wing A."

"Can't," Riley said sorrowfully. "Some restructuring going on. The access door is closed off."

"Hmm." Emma's voice, the sound of pounding on a keyboard in the background. "Then through the kitchen, down the stairs to the food storage area where you wait, come up on the side entrance. That would be even better because Pierce will be waiting on Lee Road."

Pierce's deep voice came over. "I'll text you when I'm two minutes out, Riley. Just hang in there, keep out of sight. The Sommers Group operators are brutal but smart. Stay out of their way."

No shit, Sherlock, she wanted to say, but didn't. *Play nice.* She had some remarkable people on her side. They were mapping out an escape for her. She couldn't do it on her own. The snark came from her own terror.

"Do my best. See you on Lee Road." She waited a second, to make sure her voice didn't tremble. "Please hurry."

"You got it. I'm coming for you as fast as I can."

2

Pierce Jordan shot out of the office, down the stairs, out onto the street. He was in Washington preparing for negotiations for a new DOD contract for ASI, but he was using the offices of Black Inc., a company his company cooperated with often.

One of the Genius Squad of women back in Portland had recently saved Jacob Black's life and any ASI person was golden in Black's eyes. The Washington DC Black Inc. branch had strict instructions to help Pierce in any way it could and he had to beat the helpfulness back with a stick.

But now he really needed their help and they came through in spades. He quickly explained what he needed and a few minutes later, a car pulled up. The driver got out, holding open the door. Pierce got in.

It looked like a very normal car, not high-end. The color of dirt, no shiny bits. Nothing to catch the eye. But it was armored, had run-flat tires and could go from zero to 100 in ten seconds.

He nodded to the Black Inc. operator, who said, "We're getting set up right now. The switch will be in the Garrett Tunnel. The safe house will be in the GPS of the new car and when you arrive, it will be wiped from the GPS record." He slapped the roof. "Good luck."

Pierce nodded. The door closed with a bank vault *whump!* And he took off.

There was one goal—to get to the National Surveillance Office in Chantilly as fast as humanly possible. He was following what was happening there over his phone, through the dark web connection Riley established with her friends in Portland. He focused fiercely on driving fast without being pulled over. Any speeding tickets would be absorbed by Black Inc., but would slow him down.

All he could think about was Riley.

In the crosshairs of the Sommers Group.

When he first heard that operatives from the Sommers Group were targeting Riley, he'd broken out in a cold sweat. He'd faced danger many times. He'd been a SEAL, for fuck's sake. Under live fire, in training, his heart rate never rose above 80. He always kept his cool. Except now.

Because they weren't gunning for him, or his trained teammates. They were gunning for a smart lady who could out-think them, no problem, but not outgun and outrun them. And who sure as hell couldn't out-fight them. He felt that to his very core.

He knew the Sommers guys, and they could be brutal and ruthless. They wouldn't think twice about hurting or shooting a woman.

Pierce had never seen Riley in person, but he'd seen photos with her best friends Felicity, Hope and Emma. The affection the women held for each other rose up off the photo.

Four fabulous-looking women. Felicity, Hope and Emma were good- looking, but Riley—she was spectacularly beautiful. Ice blonde, light gray eyes, elegantly slender. She just shone on the photos. And for someone so smart, working in the field of security, she had a softness to her eyes, not the hard, cynical look so many had. The price for keeping secrets and for working in a field where bad things sometimes happened.

Like now.

Where she was being hunted by mercenaries known for their ruthlessness.

He pressed on the accelerator, taking a corner on two wheels.

If the police came after him, he'd just outrun them, because time was running out and he was terrified of finding a gorgeous corpse at the end of his run.

He could hear Hope and Emma giving her instructions over the open line, though he didn't intervene. There was nothing he could do beyond what he was already doing—racing like an arrow to her.

Hope and Emma—and Felicity when she wasn't in the bathroom throwing up—were guiding her, blanking out video cameras in a nonobvious way, following the movements of the Sommers operators.

Riley could have done this herself, but she said her magic computer was in her apartment. On the job, NRO employees were not allowed to bring their own electronic devices into the building. Pierce inferred that Riley had managed to copy some data onto a thumb drive, which she gave to a man who was now dead.

She couldn't hack into the security system with just her cell phone.

But her friends back at ASI could. Oh yeah.

Pierce had actually never seen the women of the IT department say something couldn't be done, when asked. The Queens of IT. Somehow, they always found a way. And they'd found a way to follow where the Sommers operators were at all times. Riley had to get out of the building just in time to meet him on Lee Road.

Pierce gave a quick glance to the GPS. "Eight minutes out," he muttered to Hope and Emma and heard them repeat that to Riley. She had eight minutes to make her way down to the ground floor and come out the side entrance, where the blacked-out video cameras wouldn't be noticed.

"Red Team has split up," Hope announced. Shit. That was bad news. While the Sommers operators were moving as a team, Riley had more chances of slipping out. Three operators splitting up decreased her chances of getting out unnoticed. They could cover three times the ground.

Fuck. He increased his speed, shooting past red lights when he thought he could. He'd been a combat driving instructor, and trusted himself and the vehicle, driving as fast as possible because these douchebros had already killed one person and were gunning for Riley.

Not if he could stop it.

He accelerated a bit more.

"Five minutes." Hope and Emma relayed the information. "We looped the cameras in the western stairwell, she's coming down now. She's locking the stairwell doors as she comes down."

Smart cookie. Sommers guys were ruthless but they also would not want to attract too much attention. The geniuses back at ASI would definitely have not cut out the video cameras where the Sommers men passed through the NSO. They were leaving behind a ton of evidence. So whatever it was they wanted from Riley, or wanted to stop Riley from doing, they were willing to risk big.

They wanted her, badly.

"Coming up on the building," he muttered. There was a straightaway and he poured on the speed, shooting past other cars as if they were standing still. "Tell Riley—" He leaned forward a little. "Never mind, I see her! Tell her to cross to Lee Road."

He could see her cock her head, listening to her friends on the other side of the country. Her head snapped up and she saw him, speeding along the highway that fronted the NSO.

She was a fast runner, and she was going to meet him just as he came to the closest point.

Wow. Very fast runner. She looked like an Olympian runner, all blurry speed and grace.

It was going to work.

"Pierce." Hope's grim voice came over his earbuds. "The Sommers operators are racing down the stairwell. All together. They've located Riley. I don't know how."

Fuck!

There were bollards on the access road. He couldn't get closer to the building. Riley was running across an open space. Right now, it looked as big as a football field and she was totally exposed. If they were willing to shoot, they had her. Though they couldn't catch her. She had a head start and few men could run as fast as she could.

Special Forces operators were trained to run for long distances, but they weren't especially fast. Riley was *fast.*

"They're at the outside door," Hope said.

Riley was only halfway across the square.

Pierce was going to reach the square on the driver's side. Riley would have to round the car to get to the passenger side. Across the square, the big door opened and three men rushed out. Two started running after Riley, one assumed a gunman's stance, legs braced, left hand holding the right hand. With a Glock 19 in it.

Pierce stood on the brakes and turned the steering wheel, doing a 180, and reached across to open the door. He'd calculated it perfectly, the car coming to a stop, wheels smoking, exactly where Riley reached him.

She dove in and he held out his right hand with his Glock 22 and shot right over her head. The man who was shooting spun around so fast Pierce could see drops of blood floating in the air. Pierce shot again, twice, hitting the concrete right in front of the feet of the two men chasing Riley. Concrete chips shot up.

He pulled Riley's door closed, just in time to hear two *pocks!* as two bullets hit the armored door. Two seconds more and those bullets would have hit Riley.

Pierce did a 180 again. In the rear-view window he could see the two operators standing in the road, lowering their guns. Those Glocks weren't going to penetrate an armored vehicle.

Riley was curled in the passenger seat.

"Riley."

"Yes?" The face she turned up to his was sheet white.

"Fasten your seat belt."

"What?" She blinked slowly.

"Fasten your seat belt." He put command into his voice. "*Now.*"

She scrabbled, and when he heard the click of the belt engaging, he hit the accelerator.

3

During the Kosovo War, fighter jets would take off from Whiteman AFB, fly to Kosovo, drop their bombs and fly back, without ever landing. Pilots flew for thirty hours or more. They flew perfectly, bombed perfectly, landed perfectly after a day and a half of flying. They were drugged to the gills, of course, mainly on amphetamines.

Adrian Sommers often thought of them. He'd just joined the Navy and was awed at the thought of being able to fight, tirelessly, for long periods. He happened to be at Whiteman AFB on TDY when one of the pilots flew in, landed as sweetly as a baby's bottom.

Someone said the pilot had been flying for thirty-five hours, and Sommers waited to see him get out of the cockpit, expecting to see a man on his last legs, drawn and exhausted. Instead, the pilot hopped down, bright-eyed and energetic, hair wet with the sweat of wearing a helmet for so many hours, but otherwise looking great. He slapped the back of one of the mechanics and with a little group of airmen went off to have a beer.

Sommers asked one of the airmen at the hangar what kind of man could fly a fighter jet for so long and look so good at the end of it, and the man winked and said, "St. Dextroampheta-mine. Works every time."

Ever since, Sommers had been obsessed with performance-enhancing drugs. He left the military as early as he could. No money to be made in the military. Even if you made it to the top, kissing asses all the way up, the average salary was 100k a year.

Peanuts.

As soon as he could, he got out and founded a security company. He had perfect operators, too. Men who had tried out to become Navy SEALs but had to ring the bell and quit. Anyone who made it to Hell Week was pretty good. Who the fuck cared if they made it all the way? If they did make it all the way, they stayed until they retired, and were no use to Sommers. And SEALs charged top dollar.

No, the ones who almost made it, who were strong and fast and smart, under thirty—that was a Sommers operator. They were grateful, too, when he recruited them, at double the salary they'd been making. And most of them weren't too picky about following the rules.

He operated mainly abroad. There were damn few rules he had to follow, no stupid rules of engagement, as long as he got results.

He also made sure his men got whatever they needed to perform. Amphetamines, methylphenidates, creatine, anabolic steroids, even cocaine. Their performance doubled.

The money rolled in.

And then he heard about a rogue chemist, formerly working in the research lab of a big pharma company. Word had it that the chemist had come up with a formula for performance enhancers that didn't wreck the heart and wasn't addictive. He'd had a few operators drop dead of unexplained heart attacks with previous drugs. Often, though, they were in countries where the authorities weren't too particular and where bodies disappeared.

And he would give a bonus of $100K to the members of the team.

This drug wasn't like that. It operated on different principles and used different pathways. The chemist—who lost his job with the big pharma company and came to work for the Sommers group—tried to explain it, but Sommers couldn't follow and didn't care. What he cared about was productivity and, man, it just shot through the roof.

The chemist kept tinkering, happy as a pig in slop. But one day his tinkering came back to bite everyone in the ass.

Sommers had a team operating in Congo. They were supposed to stop a team from a Belgian mining multinational who apparently had found a lithium mine. There was an American prospecting team in the area who wanted to get to the mine first, stake their claim. His men had orders to ... stop the Belgian geologists. Any way they could.

There was a tight timeline, and a very nice bonus if they met it. Sommers gave the group the latest drug his chemist had nicknamed Greased Lightning, the GPS coordinates and instructions to hurry.

The men went nuts. Read the GPS coordinates wrong, came across an American research team of virologists, thought they were the Belgian geologists, and killed everyone.

It was Congo. Deep in the jungle. No one had to know. Except it turned out that during the massacre, an American satellite had filmed everything.

When Sommers heard the news, he knew he was in deepest shit. This wasn't something that could be buried or bought. It was on tape.

His men had come directly from providing security to a Moroccan general and had been in full Sommers Group uniform, so there was no doubt who had perpetrated the massacre. Sommers frantically tried gaming escape hatches, but there weren't any.

Then he remembered meeting a guy at one of the endless parties on the Washington circuit. A guy who worked at the NSO and who knew how to manipulate images.

It was a huge gamble, but Sommers had gambled before and come out on top. Turned out the guy at the NSO, a guy named Morris Sartan, was very receptive to money. Very. He was expensive, but he made the problem go away. The footage of his men attacking American scientists became footage of Chinese soldiers attacking American scientists.

Everyone knew the Chinese were everywhere in Africa. So a group of them went crazy—so what?

But it turned out that Chinese troops going nuts, attacking American scientists, even deep in the jungle, was a very big deal.

At least they didn't know those troops were Sommers Group operators. The operators weren't talking. The 'wonder drug' they'd used caused massive brain damage. It put half of them into a coma and turned the rest into drooling shells who couldn't feed themselves or tie their own shoelaces. Something about affecting the neocortex, his scientist explained in technical terms, that Sommers didn't follow.

Basically, one big whoopsie.

Sommers had just finished burying the last member of the team when his guy in the NSO, Sartan, called and said that some nosy interfering office drone named Henry Yu uncovered the deepfake. Yu had taken his findings to Sartan, who said he'd look into it and called in a strike team. Sommers sent his three best men and they took care of Yu. And then Sartan said that the person who actually uncovered the deepfake was a young woman. Riley Robinson.

Sommers sent his team after her, sure that a gunshot would take care of her like it took care of Yu. They'd staged it as a suicide. Lots of suicides this year at the NSO. Something in the water?

However, in the meantime, with the threat of a real shooting war on the horizon, Pentagon contracts started rolling in. He'd fallen into the shit and come out smelling like a rose. All he needed to do was get rid of one woman.

But somehow this young woman, a computer expert, a fucking lady nerd, evaded his men, ran into a car and disappeared.

Right now, the fortunes of Adrian Sommers and of the Sommers Group depended on this bitch not being alive. He had to find her. Eliminate her.

Had to.

RILEY WAS alive by a miracle and by the help of her best friends all the way across the continent. They guided her through the building while she was blind. Personal laptops were not allowed in the building. NSO laptops had transponders—she didn't dare grab hers. She had to go on the run with only her cell which, thank God, she'd turned into a satphone that couldn't be tracked.

Hope and Emma kept her informed every step of the way where the Sommers soldiers were, otherwise she would never have had a chance, particularly after the men split up. Once, a Sommers guy walked right by her, not five feet away. She had flattened herself inside a door niche in a cross corridor and he never noticed. Hope and Emma also kept her away from groups of people because you never knew.

Slowly, creeping down temporarily empty corridors, hiding in bathrooms, taking stairwells, she made her way to the ground floor.

Her heart beating wildly the entire time.

Hope and Emma also kept her informed on the man racing toward her to rescue her. Pierce Jordan. Good guy. Emma's boyfriend's best friend. Solid. Reliable. Skilled.

She needed that more than anything. She was solid and reliable and skilled too, and look where that got her. Running for her life.

No, this Pierce apparently was skilled in exotic things like sniping and urban warfare, and had even been undercover with terrorists for over a year. Cool under fire.

Yeah. She needed someone who could keep his cool because she was burning up with anxiety and terror.

Riley was very aware that she was sitting on a bomb. There were enormous interests in play. And she had proof of criminal activity on the part of one of the most powerful security companies on earth.

A none-too-scrupulous security company, as Hope's boyfriend unhelpfully added. "Scumbags" is the way Luke Reynolds put it.

Pierce had skills but so presumably did the Sommers Group people. And they were gunning for her, personally. Armed men, unscrupulous men, men who'd killed her boss like a bug—just swatted him away—those men were after her.

She was smart and resourceful in her profession but in terms of self-defense, of evading trained killers, she had no skills whatsoever.

So Hope and Emma and Felicity's friend was speeding his way to her, but he wasn't here yet. Hope kept her informed on his ETA. Once she reached the ground floor, she had to stay out of sight because he was ten minutes out.

Then five.

Then two.

One.

"Go," Hope whispered, and Riley opened the side entrance and slipped out.

An intake of breath in her earbuds and Emma yelled, "Go Riley! The Sommers guys are on the ground floor! *Gogogo!*"

She shot from the building like a bat out of hell because that was one skill she did have. She was a runner. She ran marathons. She could run a four-minute mile.

She'd seen the men up on the fourth floor. They looked terrifying. Strongly built, heavily armed, with body armor. But those builds, and that kind of equipment, slowed you down.

She could outrun them all.

She couldn't outrun a bullet, though.

Riley was halfway across the open square in front of the NSO's main building when she heard male voices, shouting.

They were immediately drowned out by the sound of a supercharged engine, growling. Coming fast. She looked to the right where a car was coming at the speed of light. Certainly faster than it looked capable of doing. She chanced a look over her shoulder and her knees nearly buckled.

The men had fanned out and were running after her. They also had guns up and out. They'd probably rather catch her than shoot her, particularly since they were out in the open, but they'd shoot if they had to.

Pierce Jordan, the man sent by her friends, was coming from the wrong side. He'd be at her position in a second or two, but she'd have to run around the car to get to the passenger side. Quite enough time to be gunned down.

Then there was a squeal of brakes added to the growling engine and the car neatly turned, tires smoking, 180°, until she was facing the passenger side. It was beautifully timed and like magic, the passenger side door opened.

"Get in!" the driver urged, and she didn't need to be told twice. She dove into the footwell and he reached across to pull the door closed, not before getting off a few shots over her head.

The car hadn't come to a complete stop.

She scrambled into the seat and cried out when she heard a ping. Looking back, she could see one of the Sommers men slightly crouched, both hands holding a mean-looking big black gun. He took another shot and it pinged off the door.

The car, which didn't look like much, was armored. And thank God, because...

"Seat belt," the driver said, voice cold and remote.

"What?" Her head whipped around to him.

"Seat belt," he repeated. "*Now.*"

They had armed men, former soldiers, gunning for them, and he was worried about *traffic rules?*

But he'd saved her life and was still was saving her life. So, she sat in the passenger seat and reached over for the belt.

As soon as she heard the snick of the seat belt, something— some gigantic force—punched her in the chest and the landscape outside the windows was replaced by a blur.

The vehicle was more like a rocket than a car as it shot down the street.

Riley couldn't catch her breath enough to scream as they took a corner almost on two wheels and shot past other cars. It was a miracle she wasn't hearing sirens as police cars raced after them. But very few police cars could keep up.

She was frozen with fear, almost unable to breathe. It felt like there'd be a pile-up any second, and they'd have to pry her dead body from the wreckage with the Jaws of Life.

With difficulty, she moved her head so she could see the driver. Pierce Jordan. Neither Hope nor Emma had said he was insane. He sure didn't look insane. This was the kind of speed maybe a suicidal driver would have, planning on driving over the edge of a cliff. Sporting a rictus grin, like Slim Pickens whooping and waving his cowboy hat as he rode the missile to Armageddon. Or like Thelma and Louise, one last *fuck you* to life.

But no. He looked normal—albeit very handsome—as he drove. Face composed, set, totally concentrated on the road.

Well, yeah. At any moment they were going to crash and burn, so of course he was focused. She turned her face toward the windshield so she could at least see her death approaching.

In her terror, she hadn't noticed where they were going and was now totally lost. Her agency was in generic suburbia where the streets all looked alike. She'd only been working for less than a year at the National Surveillance Office, and basically knew the road from her place to work and back.

This wasn't it.

Where were they going at this breakneck speed? Pierce must have an idea because he didn't waver at any of the intersections he sped through.

Well, wherever they were going, she had no say in the matter. So she did the only thing she could do—hold on to the door handhold so she could pull back if they looked like they were about to crash.

Just like she did in planes. She hated flying, so she spent most flights holding on to the arm rest white-knuckled, so she could keep the plane up if the engines went out.

"Get ready," Pierce said unexpectedly.

"What?" She turned her head to look at him. He was playing the brakes and the gear shift like a musical instrument as they slowed down. Why were they slowing down? Had they reached their destination? They were entering a tunnel, so how could that be a destination?

Pierce had pulled over to the extreme right, basically in the break-down lane, and had slowed down dramatically. They were travelling at the speed of a person walking. Ahead of them was some kind of truck, travelling as slowly as they were. He slowed even further and, surprisingly, reached over to unbuckle her seat belt. "Get out," he said.

She bit her lip. *Get out?* But, again, he didn't look crazy and didn't sound crazy, so she did as he asked. The car was moving so slowly, it was just a question of stepping out carefully. He exited from his side at the exact same moment she did.

And a man from behind them stepped toward the car at the same time. She hadn't noticed him. Pierce signaled to her to get into the car behind them. A black SUV. The windows were clear, but for some reason she couldn't see inside the SUV. The man had slid out from the driver's side and Pierce had slid in, slickly done. The car was moving so slowly it was easy to get into the passenger seat.

The man who'd been the driver in the car rushed to the car they'd been in and slid into the driver's seat.

They'd switched vehicles smoothly and in only a few seconds.

The car in front of them, the one they'd been in a few minutes before, drove right up into the truck, whose back panel had lowered. It drove up into the truck, the back panel lifted up, and it was as if the car had never existed. Pierce drove back into the usual lane and sped up past the truck.

They exited the tunnel and she realized that if traffic cameras had caught them going into the tunnel, they wouldn't catch their vehicle coming out. It would take them time to figure out what had happened, if they managed to figure it out at all. Plus they would have no way to know which vehicle they were in.

Pierce was driving the speed limit in their ordinary-looking SUV that was somehow impervious to outside eyes. When they exited the tunnel, Riley turned around. Four cars back, the truck with the car inside exited from the tunnel. Any exam of the traffic cameras would show that the car they'd escaped in had disappeared.

For the moment, they were safe.

Riley took in a deep breath and turned to the man who'd made it happen. "That was neatly done. Thanks."

Now that they were driving at a normal speed, Pierce had lost that remote, hard look. He turned briefly and smiled. "Sure. I had help."

She blinked at the smile.

Oh my God. The man was *handsome*! She'd sort of known it because she'd seen a couple of photos, and some tiny part of her lizard brain had noticed his looks when he rescued her, but the rest of her brain had been in survival mode and it just remained there, like a little factoid.

The sun was shining, mercenaries were trying to kill her, Pierce Jordan was hot.

Part of it was the smile. Genuine, warm, unexpected. The complete opposite of the robotic expressionless face he'd had before, when driving them to safety at a billion miles an hour.

His features were sharp, intriguing. Coupled with blue-black hair and deep blue eyes—wow. He had an amazing physique, too. Tall, broad-shouldered, athletic. Nature didn't usually grace people with many gifts and she would have thought he'd be limited in the brains department, but no. He was apparently really smart, or so Hope said, when she told Riley she'd be in good hands. And good at his job. Apparently, he won medals for something no one could know about.

And had engineered an amazing getaway.

"I imagine the video cams in the tunnel have been turned off."

He flashed another grin and it was almost too much. She was still shaky from the escape, from having armed men hunting her like a deer and she nearly said *don't do that. Don't smile, you're giving me the bends. I can't take it.*

Which was crazy, of course. She was filled with adrenaline. Her hands were shaking badly and she folded one over the other in an attempt to stop them from trembling.

Pierce's blue eyes seemed to notice everything. He put his big hand over hers and the shaking stilled.

She looked down at his hand over hers. He'd saved her life and he was still saving her. "Sorry," she whispered.

"No worries." Oh God, overkill. For the first time she noticed his voice. Dark and warm and deep. A voice to fall into. "Anyone would tremble after what you've just been through."

Not him, though. He was steady as a rock.

"And you're right. Your genius friends turned off the cameras in the tunnel. It was their idea because to get to the safe house, we have to drive through some stretches that are full of private video cameras and there wouldn't be time to turn them all off. So it was their idea to switch vehicles. Black Inc. made the truck happen."

A lot of resources to keep her safe. And a lot of people working to keep her safe. She had to do her part. Her hands stilled.

She had to focus on what he was saying.

"We're going to a safe house?" He'd managed to organize a safe house?

Pierce's hands were back on the steering wheel. He was looking straight ahead but she had the feeling he was fully concentrated on her. She always found it hard to carry on a conversation while driving, because conversations interested her more than taking a car from A to B.

That killer smile again. "Yeah. Courtesy of Black Inc. And their safe houses are notoriously nice." The smile vanished. "You have some seriously nasty people after you, Riley."

She looked down at her hands again. "Yes, I know."

He reached over to squeeze her hands again. His own hands were very warm. Though it was a warm day, she felt chilled everywhere except her hands.

He glanced over at her while his hand returned to the steering wheel. "We're almost there."

She blinked. She had paid no attention whatsoever to where they were going. Her training was to remain inside her own head at all times, and she rarely noticed the outside world. Of course, she was usually in her dim cubicle far removed from the outside world, so it wasn't a handicap. But now it was. She was ashamed to say she had no idea where they were.

It was a suburban area, full of nice houses and a few upscale condo buildings. Affluent, but not super rich. Washington, DC was full of places like this. They could be anywhere.

"Sorry to ask, but... where are we? I've only been in Washington less than a year and I basically know the route from my place to work. I'm totally lost. Sorry."

"Don't be sorry. We're in Alexandria and ... we're here."

He turned into a driveway and stopped at a gate. He tapped in a password on his cell and the gate opened smoothly, sliding to one side rather than opening out.

The gate closed as soon as they were through. Pierce drove into an alleyway by the side of the house. It had netting on top and was enclosed by netting.

"Cool," she observed. "Drone proof."

"Yep. Wait here."

He went around to the back of the vehicle and pulled out a big duffle bag. It looked heavy, but he lifted it easily, and came around to the passenger side. He opened her door, holding out a hand to help her down.

She was about to protest that she didn't need a helping hand, when her knees buckled. She didn't fall because his hand was right there, holding her up, strong and sure.

She stiffened her knees and dropped his hand. "Whoa. Sorry about that."

He gave her an easy smile and put a hand on her back. "I keep telling you, nothing to be sorry about. You've got people after you, trying to kill you. That'd be enough to dent anyone's mojo." He kept the hand there, gently, as he ushered her into the side entrance of the safe house.

It was nice. Riley had no idea how long they were going to stay here—the future was this blank, featureless desert. She was a planner, always had been. Her parents swayed with the tides, but she never had.

But right now? It was impossible to predict the next five minutes, let alone the next five days or weeks, so she didn't even try.

Pierce directed her to a comfortable sofa and she collapsed onto it, surprised at her weakness. She wasn't weak, she was strong. This horrible situation was sapping her of herself. Then: "What?"

Pierce had said something and she only heard the tail end of it.

"I said, what can I give you to steady your nerves? There's every type of tea, black or herbal, every flavor of coffee, and a couple of excellent brandies and whiskies.

Oh man, a whiskey sounded really nice, but not a good idea. "A tea would be nice. Black tea with milk. No sugar." She looked up at Pierce. Not expressionless now. He looked reassuring and a little worried. About her. She wasn't used to anyone worrying about her. She'd made her own way in the world for a long time now. This man clearly had the wrong impression of her.

She straightened up in the sofa, lifted her chin, steadied her hands in her lap. There. That was the Riley Robinson everyone knew.

"Here." A steaming cup of black tea appeared on a tray with a small pitcher of milk. She leaned over and drew in a breath. It smelled divine. Earl Grey. There was a plate with English shortbread. The Full Monty—English Xanax. He himself had a cup of coffee, black.

"I don't have a drop of English blood in me, but this is programmed to soothe anyone's nerves." He smiled at her.

She smiled back. "It's a superior safe house if you have English shortbread and fresh milk."

He sipped. She could smell the coffee—some rich brew, probably arabica. "You have no idea. This is a Black Inc. safe-house and it practically comes with masseuses. There's a fridge full of fresh food, a list of take-out restaurants close by, a full wine cellar, and freshly laundered sheets and towels. And they carry a stock of basic clothes in various sizes, plus pajamas. You'll find something that fits you in your room. And basic toiletries."

"They think of everything." Now that she was safe and they weren't flying at the speed of light, she was starting to get her bearings. And realizing she'd left the office with only a tiny fanny pack. She had nothing. And she particularly didn't have a computer. *Her* computer. It made her feel naked.

"They certainly do." Pierce leaned toward her. "Listen, Riley. I am not entirely certain what this is about. The only thing I know from your genius friends is that what you found out is deadly serious, with serious national security implications. If you don't mind, I'd like to ask Jacob Black to come in for your debrief. He can be here soon and you could shower and change if you want to, in the meantime. That way you won't have to repeat your story twice."

She was going to have to repeat her story over and over again, but it was nice of him to try to spare her.

A huge weight lifted from her shoulders. She was choking on the responsibility she felt. Right now, with Henry Yu dead, she was the only person in the world who knew that the country might be going to war over a lie.

Jacob Black was very welcome.

Jacob Black was a legend, a man intimately connected with the military and with serious ties to Congress. He would definitely know what to do. She could tip this problem right into his thoroughly capable hands.

She exhaled. "Oh God, yes!" She put the tea cup back in its saucer and was horrified to hear it rattle. Just like her heart was still rattling around in her chest. "And you can brief your bosses back in Portland, right?" Pierce's company wasn't as large and powerful as Black Inc., but it was still a highly respected security company, one of the best in the country. "The more people who know, the better."

"And the safer you'll be." Pierce rose and she looked up at him. He was very tall. Usually she didn't like tall men. They often used their height to intimidate. But Pierce didn't. It just seemed to be an attribute of the man, like broad shoulders and big hands. He was tall, but it didn't bother her. He held out a hand and she stood. It was awful that she was grateful for the hand.

He gently grasped her shoulders and pointed to a door. "That's your room. You have your own bathroom and you'll find everything you need in there. Clothes and toiletries." He turned her around, looking her deeply in the eyes. He hesitated a moment, as if to give weight to his words. "You're safe now, Riley. I want you to know that. To feel that."

"I do. I feel safe. Particularly since I'm not in a car going 200 miles an hour."

He gave a crack of laughter. "I was taking it easy. The car doesn't look like much, I know, but it can hit 200. We were only going 150, tops. And you were never in any danger. I'm a combat driving instructor."

It had felt like she was going to die at any moment, but she realized now that she'd been in good hands.

He turned her back around. "Now go," he said gently. "And we'll talk about this when Black gets here."

Somehow Pierce realized that she really needed a break. She'd been on red alert for hours. One of the best ways she knew to relax a little was to take a shower. Standing under falling water had always been her way to destress. That and climbing rocks, but there were no rocks here at the moment.

She stood under the waterfall showerhead, one hand against the sandstone-tiled wall and emptied her head. So many questions, so many decisions, so many facts to sift through, so many probabilities, so many geopolitical factors, such dire consequences ... she couldn't deal with them all at once, so she thought of nothing at all. Merely luxuriated in the feel of hot water sliding over her body, feeling her heart rate slide back to its usual sixty beats per minute.

The room really did have everything. A comfortable-looking, freshly made king-size bed. A closet with sports clothes of varying colors on hangers. Many items were in her size. A big dresser with sweaters and tees, brand new underwear, pajamas. On the nightstand a bottle of water, aspirin, ibuprofen, dark-blue nail polish, two jars of excellent moisturizer and in the nightstand drawer ... *ohmygod*. Condoms! Lots and lots of condoms!

Face red, she hastily pushed them to the back of the top drawer because the last thing she needed right now was condoms. Sex was the furthest thing from her mind.

Except ... she'd had to run for her life. At the NSO it had

been so close. Armed gunmen had come for her, and they already had the scent of blood in their nostrils. They'd wanted her dead and it was a miracle they hadn't succeeded. She could be dead right now, cold and gone, just like Henry Yu. Lying on some slab in some morgue, with a toe tag, forever dead.

Instead, she was alive. Super alive, in fact. She tingled with life from head to toe and so ... well ... sex was actually *not* the furthest thing from her mind.

Except of course it had to vie with fear for her life.

That wild car ride, for example. She'd been terrified. She'd never ridden at that speed before in her life. She was braced for a horrific accident that would crush her as the car crumpled against a lamppost or another vehicle. But at the same time, there was a part of her that hadn't been scared at all, because Pierce had looked utterly in control at all times. Still, she'd felt a jolt of adrenaline getting out of the car because she'd survived the ride.

She was *alive.*

Life pulsed in every cell of her body. Heat rushed through her. It wasn't just the hot water running down her body, it was a heat that came from within. Like someone had thrown a switch and turned her on inside.

Oh my God, Pierce Jordan turned her on. That was it.

This was a really bad moment to get a crush on a guy. Riley didn't do crushes. She waited a long time, studying a man, before becoming interested. And most men weren't that interesting. If they were intellectually interesting, they weren't physically interesting. And vice versa.

But Pierce was absolutely fascinating. His dramatic rescue. His being able to organize a car switch, a safe house, was ... well, sexy. A guy who knew how to get things done. Who knew how to operate in the world. Her friends in Portland said he was very smart, though she hadn't heard more than a couple of words come out of his mouth. But he looked and acted smart and that was enough.

Plus he was immensely attractive. Good-looking, but definitely not vain.

This was strange, too, because Riley wasn't turned on by men's looks. She wasn't that shallow, or so she'd always thought.

And yet, here she was. Turned on by a handsome man. A very handsome man. Tall, dark and handsome, a walking cliché. But it turned out he also happened to be competent and brave, and had stepped forward immediately when her friends asked him to help her. He hadn't been fazed at all by men shooting at him. He'd even shot *back*.

She didn't have enough trouble, with her boss having been killed, with killers now after her? She had to throw inappropriate feelings into the mix?

Riley sighed as she got dressed. None of this was easy. But she'd been doing hard things, on her own, all her life. She pushed open the door into the living room and immediately two big men stood up, in unison.

Riley took a step back. Why did they rise? Were they planning on going somewhere and were just waiting until she finished her shower to tell her?

And then it hit her. Old-fashioned manners. Men rising when a lady entered the room. Though to be honest, she'd only ever read that in novels. She inhabited a world where all the male etiquette her nerd colleagues ever knew was to keep their pants zipped and shoelaces tied.

She nearly said, "At ease, men." Because they both looked almost at parade rest. As she moved toward them, they both sat down again.

It was the first leisurely look she'd had of Pierce. They'd been so busy saving her that she hadn't had a chance to get a really good look at him. The general impression had been big and handsome. It was now reinforced. He was tall, lean, and broad, with sinewy muscles showing through the tee. And he was incredibly good-looking. Lavishly so. Deep blue eyes fringed by black eyelashes. Sharp cheekbones, straight aquiline nose, chiseled jaw, full lips, now compressed in a straight line.

And that body, broad and lean, arrow-straight. He looked like sex and sanctuary, both. It was hard for her not to rush straight to him, because her feeling of safety rose the closer she was to him.

But she didn't rush to him because of the second man. Jacob Black. The man was famous, but not because he courted fame. His photo sometimes appeared online and in the papers, but never posed photos. Always of him coming or going. The man was wealthy beyond words, his company, Black Inc., incredibly successful.

But it wasn't his wealth that you noticed first. Most wealthy men dressed for success, in cashmere and linen and silk. Not Jacob Black. He had on a black tee shirt, a dark, untucked cotton shirt and black jeans. Black combat boots. Dark, harsh features. He hadn't shaved and looked tired. He might have just come from a mission.

The most important aspect about him was power. He gave off waves of power, like a king or an emperor. Every line of his body shimmered with power. He wasn't looking happy, either. Black eyebrows were drawn over black eyes and his mouth was downturned.

For a moment, Riley was frightened. Not frightened, not really. Surely, Pierce wouldn't let any harm come to her from Jacob Black? If nothing else, Felicity, Hope and Emma would be on his case, big time.

No, Jacob Black wasn't going to attack her, but he was seriously angry with something or someone.

Please, God, not with her.

His black eyes had followed her as she approached, narrowing to dark slits.

Pierce brushed her arm. "Riley, I want to introduce you to Jacob Black, of Black Inc. My company works often with his company, and he is a personal friend. Jacob, this is Riley Robinson. She works at the NSO."

Black stuck out a huge, calloused hand. "And she is friends with ASI's genius women, right?

"Right," Pierce nodded.

Then Black's entire face underwent a metamorphosis as a smile lit up his harsh features. It was the kind of smile a pirate would make just before ordering someone to walk the plank, but it was a smile.

"Your friends are amazing. I owe my life to one of them, Emma Holland. Consider me and the resources of my company at your complete disposal. Delighted to meet you, Ms. Riley." Emma had helped find a bomb set to go off at a meeting of top-level security experts. Jacob Black had organized the security forces. If not for Emma and her fiancé, Raul, Jacob Black wouldn't be here. He'd be guarding the perimeter of Heaven.

But having Jacob Black and his company, and Pierce Jordan and his incredible company at her disposal ... wow.

And yet it might not be enough.

"Nice to meet you, too."

He engulfed her hand with his, shook it once, and withdrew. She'd been scared that he'd pull a macho stunt, crushing her hand, showing his strength, but he didn't. He simply stood, smiling down at her from somewhere near the ceiling.

Was she supposed to ... "Please." She swallowed heavily. "Call me Riley."

"Then you must call me Jacob." She blinked at the thought of calling one of the most powerful men in America, in the *world*, by his first name. It felt unnatural.

"Hmm."

"Let's sit down," Pierce suggested, "and we can talk about Riley's ... issue. I don't know too much about it. ASI and our IT department pressed the emergency button and sent me to pick up Riley at the NSO, but there wasn't time for a briefing. I have little intel."

"Good thing you came, too," she said. "Otherwise I'd be dead." She sat down at the end of a sectional couch. It was very comfortable.

Jacob Black's head turned at that, but he didn't say anything. He sat down in an armchair perpendicular to the couch.

Pierce was still standing. "Before we start, does anyone want anything? Coffee? Tea? Water?"

"Coffee. Black." She would have guessed that was Jacob Black's drink of choice.

"Tea. Milk. Again. Please," she said. "And I'm going to need a laptop. I left everything of mine behind at the office."

In a moment, Pierce had her cup of tea and two cups of pitch-black coffee on the coffee table. He disappeared for a second and came out with the latest version of a laptop produced by a big company.

He set the laptop in front of her and surprised her by sitting right next to her.

She opened the laptop and winced. Then sighed.

Pierce sighed too. "Emma told me you'd turn your nose up at the laptop."

She side-eyed him as she went to the browser, torn between snobbishness at the inferior hardware and software, and gratitude that he was doing everything in his power to help her.

"Hmmm."

Pierce looked mournful. "It's the latest version. Costs a lot. Has a pretty fancy shell. Has a big memory."

She side-eyed him again. The laptop was crap. She and her

friends were continuously testing beta models of ambitious companies, and even the lowliest beta would leave this POS in the dust. But no use saying that.

She glanced up, out the window. The sun was starting to set and the sun's rays beamed horizontally into the window. Out of the corner of her eye she saw the flatscreen TV over the fireplace, tuned to an all-news channel with muted sound.

"Whoa!" Riley sat up straight.

Pierce and Jacob Black swiveled their heads.

She pointed at the flat screen TV, where a female news anchor with old fashioned helmet hair was talking against a background of aircraft carriers. The chyron at the bottom said, *Two carriers of the 7th fleet sailing to Taiwan.* "Turn the sound on!"

Pierce touched a button on a remote and the sound came on.

"... though no official statements have been made by the Ministry of Foreign Affairs of the People's Republic of China, unofficial sources say that a General Alert has gone out to the People's Liberation Army Navy, the lowest level of alert, the equivalent of our Defcon IV. The top brass has been meeting inside the headquarters in Beijing nonstop for the past 24 hours. To recap, days after an attack on American scientists in Congo ..."

The famous photo showed. Men in lab coats in a clearing in the jungle, Chinese attackers just emerging from the jungle, weapons out.

Riley muted the TV again.

"OK," she said. "You guys have been watching this, right?"

Both men nodded.

"It's all fake. All a lie, every second of it, from beginning to end." She pulled Pierce's laptop to her. "Watch."

4

Pierce knew in very broad strokes what was happening, but it was news to Jacob Black. He wasn't the kind of guy to rear back in surprise. Special Forces operators—and Black had been one of the best—never showed surprise. But he could sense Black's intense interest.

Riley was pounding away at the keyboard of a laptop he was sure she disdained. But she hadn't said anything, even though he was certain she was thinking it. She was intensely focused on whatever it was she was doing, and Black was focused on her, after she'd thrown her little bombshell.

He was certain Black was involved at the highest levels in the war-gaming that was going on all over Washington and in the capitals of the world. Riley had just thrown him for a loop.

So Pierce had a little window of opportunity to study her. Her photo on the corkboard of the IT office back in Portland had intrigued him no end. Four beautiful women, but he had eyes only for the one in the middle. Good thing, too, because Felicity, Hope and Emma were spoken for by his brothers Metal, Luke and Raul. If he was fascinated by any of them, he'd never have acted on it. But he wasn't. He was fascinated by Riley, the most beautiful of them all. Elegant and aloof, never laughing in the photos he'd seen, but always smiling. Something a little sad in those amazing eyes.

She'd completely forgotten about him and even about Black as she was diving into some kind of database. The other women did that too, his brothers reported. Simply disappeared into their computer screens when something intrigued them or worried them.

Riley would be completely taken by this issue. A war was brewing between the two major superpowers of the world, and she took it seriously. He took it seriously too, while also appreciating how incredibly appealing Riley was, super-focused. She'd been appealing running toward him outside the National Surveillance Office, too. Graceful and *fast.*

"Okay," Riley said and he shook himself, trying to get his head out of his ass. Now was not the time to obsess over Riley running.

She turned the laptop's screen so they could all see.

Riley folded her hands in her lap. "The first thing I have to say is that I pulled the images you're going to see from a cache in the dark web, where I put them. It is totally illegal for NRO employees to keep sat images for personal use. You are free to report me to the authorities, but you need to see these."

Pierce was silent, and so was Black. She thought they'd report her to the authorities? For something like this? He'd rather tear out his own throat, and Black would, too.

She gave a sigh. "Okay. What you are about to see are images taken from Scorpius, which has a Moliya-style orbit, an elliptical orbit. It's essentially a data relay satellite, intercepting and routing data from other satellites, worldwide. Which means it intercepts data from unusual latitudes and longitudes. It will eventually monitor every point on Earth.

"We were sent a video to analyze two days ago, and it was this."

She pressed a button and Pierce finally saw the entire thing and not clips that had been on the news. It was horrifying. He watched as soldiers of the PLA attacked unsuspecting scientists in a particularly brutal fashion. One scientist was even clubbed to death. White letters in the top right-hand corner gave the date, the time of day, time elapsed, the GPS coordinates, putting the attack in the empty heart of the Democratic Republic of Congo. As remote as the far side of the moon.

The video lasted almost 12 minutes, then the satellite moved on, though the killing continued. It was unusual in its ferocity, as if the Chinese soldiers had a personal beef with the scientists. At one point, a soldier lifted his face to the sky and howled silently.

It made goosebumps rise on his arms. Pierce was a soldier, had been all his adult life. He was used to battle. This wasn't battle, it was slaughter. The soldiers could easily have just rounded up the scientists, then destroyed the scientific equipment, if that was what they wanted. But they were hell-bent on destruction, frenzied. Intent on slaughter.

It was a provocation, and could lead to war.

Pierce met Black's dark gaze. He was disturbed, too, and of course understood the implications as well as he did.

Riley continued. "As far as anyone knows, PLA soldiers viciously attacked and murdered a peaceful American party of scientists. Killed them and destroyed their equipment. We all know that China is very active in Africa and has an interest in minerals and rare earth elements there. So we're looking at a clear provocation."

Pierce and Black nodded.

Riley pressed another button, then used the track pad to move around the video, which she had stilled. The trackpad allowed her to blow up elements.

"Well, it's all a fake. Look here," she commanded, and Pierce and Black both peered at the image. One of the Chinese soldiers holding a weapon. He studied it and looked at Black, who shrugged.

"Look at his hands."

Pierce did, then shrugged. They were hands. Holding a QBZ-191 assault rifle, the service rifle of the People's Liberation Army and the People's Armed Police.

"Count the fingers." With a glance at Black, Pierce leaned forward again then frowned. "Whoa."

"Wrong number, right?" Riley asked. "He has six fingers on each hand. Two other soldiers have the same. Do you know why?"

"They've been breeding soldiers in a lab and got the finger gene wrong?" Black wondered.

Riley smiled briefly. Oh man, she should smile more often. That smile broke through that sad aura that surrounded her. And you noticed her extraordinary beauty.

"No. It's because deepfake programs have trouble with fingers, because they have less data on hands than they do on faces. They're working on it, and in a year, all deepfakes will be perfect and we'll be in trouble. Or since AI works so fast, maybe the next iteration next month will be perfect."

Black sat back, looking troubled. "This is a deepfake video?"

"Yes, sir," she said. "It's been expertly altered. The original is quite different."

He frowned.

"Indeed, Mr. Bl ... Jacob. It hardly bears thinking about, yeah?"

"There are elements in the Pentagon who are gaming going to war over this."

War. With China. The ultimate nightmare. Because Pierce

knew that it wasn't a given that we'd win. And what was left of the US after war would be devastation and chaos.

"It would be a huge tragedy because there's more," she said, and tapped on the key pad. "Deepfakes are produced using an iterative process. I'm very interested in imagery and I developed an app to deep dive. I was able to peel away the layers and get to the original video, which is this."

Again she tapped a button and the screen came alive. It was the same scene, only it wasn't PLA soldiers but Western soldiers. Wearing uniforms with a black and gold symbol on their shoulders. They watched in silence. Pierce hadn't seen this before. Knowing those were soldiers on our side, viciously killing American scientists made him heartsick.

"Those are operators working for the Sommers Group," Pierce said, stunned, and Black nodded. Well, duh. Black knew that logo as well as he did. But he was taken completely aback. The Sommers Group was a well-known security company, smaller than Black Inc. and ASI, but very successful, even if they had a rep for hiring cowboy operators and for skirting the line of legality.

But this? Wholesale slaughter?

"So we are looking at what? American operators viciously attacking an American research group? Why? It doesn't make sense. I won't insult you by asking if you're sure," Black said to Riley.

"Oh yeah," She didn't look insulted, she looked sad. "I'm sure. But it's going to be very hard to prove. And they are sweeping up after themselves. I showed this video to my boss, Henry Yu, and—" her throat constricted. It took her a moment to find her voice again. "And they killed him. A quarter of an hour after he said he was kicking this upstairs, he was dead. He kicked it, but someone kicked back, hard."

Fuck. He knew it was bad, but this was sounding worse by the minute.

"Wait." Black frowned. "Your boss was killed?"

Riley nodded, straight white-blonde hair swinging. Her eyes were shiny. "Right in the building. I don't know how they did it or how they got away with it. And the bad thing is, for the moment, all the proof I have of the creation of the deepfake is on a thumb drive I gave Henry. I don't think it was found on his body, so we can be sure that the thumb drive has been destroyed or has been hidden somewhere way beyond our reach."

Pierce touched her arm and was gratified when she leaned into him. God. Any comfort he could give, he would. "Can you replicate that thumb drive?"

He was sure she'd say yes. He'd rarely heard the Geniuses— Felicity, Hope and Emma—say no, they couldn't do something. It was always *yes, I'll move mountains to do it.* So he was surprised when she shook her head. "I can't. Or rather I could if I had my computer. But I don't. It's in my apartment."

Black indicated Pierce's laptop, the best money could buy. "This won't do it?"

She shook her head again, but this time had a *get real* expression on her face. "No. It just doesn't have the power. Or the programs."

"Can we get it for you? Can we—I don't know—link two computers together, double the computing power?"

She sighed. "It's not a question of computing power, or storage. It's more a question of programming. My computer has a couple of programs on it that this one doesn't have." She held up a hand. "And I don't have the originals to load. But let's skip over that and—" Riley stopped, mouth open, staring at the TV on the wall. Both Pierce and Black turned.

Riley's face was on the screen. Riley switched on the sound.

The news anchor was reading from a sheet. "*... Robinson, an* employee of the National Surveillance Office in Chantilly, Virginia, is wanted for questioning in connection with the murder of Henry Yu, a senior official of the NSO. The National Surveillance Office is the government agency that originally released the infamous tape of a platoon of Chinese soldiers brutally attacking a group of American scientists studying viruses in a remote region of the Democratic Republic of Congo two days ago. The video has created deep tensions between the United States and the People's Republic of China.

"Henry Yu was found dead in his office of a gunshot wound to the head. However, our sources have confirmed that the angle of the shot was difficult to square with a suicide and the gun was held in Yu's right hand, when records show he was left-handed.

"Moreover, elements within the NSO confirmed that Riley Robinson and Henry Yu were having an illicit affair."

Pierce heard Riley taking in a shocked breath.

"The prevailing theory is that Ms. Robinson, a computer imaging expert working for the NSO, was working with Mr. Yu, trying to keep the video from leaking and incriminating Chinese military, and shot Mr. Yu for reasons unknown. A falling-out among spies. Stay tuned for more on The News Today at 6."

A flurry of martial music, the news logo breaking up and reassembling in vivid colors, and the program ended.

Pierce clicked the TV off.

Riley was bone-white and shaking. She brought a trembling hand to her mouth. She looked more shocked than she had when running away from men with guns.

"I—" Her mouth opened and closed.

Whoever was orchestrating this was a genius, because if she was somehow a threat to some power, she was now not only the object of a womanhunt of professional soldiers, but also of law enforcement.

Pierce sent up a big thanks to Hope and Emma for getting him involved, because Riley was otherwise a dead woman walking. He knew from his friends back in Portland that she was super smart, genius-level. And really nice and a good friend.

But that didn't give you street smarts. Didn't ensure that you could stay alive with a lot of men with guns hunting you. Without him, without Jacob Black's backing and the safe house, she'd have been dead by now.

And a really beautiful, smart, nice woman would be gone from the earth. They didn't grow that many beautiful, smart, nice women. Pierce really wanted to keep this one safe. Not to mention the fact that Felicity, Hope and Emma loved her. If anything happened to Riley on his watch, he'd be toast.

Jacob Black leaned forward, hard face grim. "What are they talking about, Riley?"

She gave a shudder, but pulled herself together. "Henry Yu is my boss. I told you I showed him my data, he said he was going to *his* boss with it. We realized that the Sommers Group was involved. I'll tell you the whole story. But after Henry went to report what we found, I heard he'd killed himself. Henry Yu is —was—the least suicidal person on earth."

Pierce leaned forward. "Someone thought fast. There's this video that is damning, so they killed the man who was bringing it to people's attention, and blamed it on his subordinate, the one who brought it to light. Two birds with one stone. Brilliant. Framing it as a lover's spat was a stroke of genius."

"It's ridiculous," Riley said. "Henry Yu was gay."

Jacob Black's head came up. "Was that general knowledge?"

Riley blinked. "What?"

"Did everyone know Yu was gay?"

She thought. "No. I mean Henry didn't hide it, but he was a very private man, had a strict rule against mixing work and his private life. He made an exception for me, but really, it just amounted to a few after-work drinks. So, no. I don't think it was general knowledge at all."

"They didn't have time to research any of it. They came after Riley right after killing Yu."

Riley turned to Pierce. "And I'm alive, thanks to you. They came after me right away, but they failed to capture me, and decided to change the narrative." She sat up straight. Some color had come back into her face. "It won't stand up to scrutiny. And what were armed operators of the Sommers Group doing at the NSO anyway? But in the meantime, they've muddied the waters and driven me into hiding. Plus stopped anyone who knew the video was a deepfake."

Black looked at Riley. "I think now would be a good time to tell us the whole story, all of it. Down to now." He paused a moment, checked his cell. "Okay. One more person has to be called in and he's here." Black stood up and went to the door.

Standing there was Black's right-hand man, Nikolai Garin. He was huge and rough-looking. Pierce glanced quickly at Riley to make sure she didn't perceive him as a danger. But she remained calm, figuring if he and Jacob Black accepted Nikolai, he was okay.

And Nikolai was more than okay. He looked like the bad guy in a B movie, the one who swings a meat cleaver, but he was solid. Skilled, and on the side of the angels. But you definitely wanted him as a friend and not an enemy.

Black and Nikolai came back into the living room and Riley rose, as did Pierce.

"Riley, this is Nikolai Garin, a vice president at Black Inc. He has a lot of contacts abroad and has been keeping his ear close to the ground. Nikolai, this is Dr. Riley Robinson, a friend of the Queens back at ASI, and someone who has a remarkable story. I called you in because it's important for you to hear it."

"Dr. Robinson," Nikolai said and held out his huge hand. He had an unusually deep voice, and Pierce saw Riley widen her eyes for just a moment.

"Mr. Garin," she answered, taking his hand. Hers disappeared for a moment in his.

"Nikolai," he said.

"Riley," she smiled.

Nikolai took the empty armchair, and Black pressed a cut crystal glass with a few fingers of whiskey into his hand without asking what Nikolai wanted. They worked together closely every day and knew each other down to the bone. Nikolai looked at Riley. "I understand that you have some information on the current situation that—" he glanced at Black, "—changes the nature of it. Black here was really cagey, so I can't imagine what it is."

Riley nodded. "Yes, I do have information. It's a real game-changer, and flips what we think is going on." She nodded, pulled Pierce's laptop toward her. "This is a shitty laptop," she grumbled, shooting a look at him. It was the second time she'd made the point.

Pierce still wasn't offended. The women of the IT department always turned their noses up at his tech, because they had access to amazing hardware and software in beta that was essentially beamed in from the future. "Best the market provides," he said mildly.

She sighed and opened his laptop up, dove into the dark web, pulled something out. She pressed a button and what was on the computer—a dark web screen with only a long alphanumerical string in green letters—went up on the wall screen.

"Okay." Riley looked at him then at Nikolai and then at Jacob Black. "Let me bring Nikolai up to speed. As I said before, what you are about to see crossed my desk more or less by accident two days ago. At the same time, it hit a few news sites. But it didn't bubble up to the surface until yesterday. It was taken by one of our Scorpius satellites. But the NSO deals in multiple terabytes of intel a day so it took some time for it to be noticed. I imagine it was plucked out of the running feed because it met the criteria for some algos. Now watch carefully."

Pierce and Black and Nikolai leaned forward. Pierce watched very carefully because this was the beginning of what was threatening this beautiful young woman, and he needed to understand every step of it.

It was still pretty shocking, though he knew what it was and had seen it multiple times before. A few seconds of the video had been playing on every major website more or less nonstop. And most websites had a disclaimer beforehand that what they were about to show was graphic. And it was.

A massacre, brutal and swift, and at the end nothing was left alive. There were even a few animals that had been killed—two monkeys and a dog.

The quality of the recording was astounding. In a few instances, he could see arterial blood spurting.

When Riley switched it off, there was silence. Total silence, because though they were in the middle of busy Alexandria, the safe house was totally sound-proofed.

"Well?" Riley turned to Black. "What did you just see, Mr. Garin—Nikolai?"

His jaw muscles clenched. "I just saw soldiers of the Peoples Liberation Army of the PRC attack an American scientific outpost in the Democratic Republic of the Congo. I saw a PLA colonel commanding them. It was a vicious and unprovoked attack on a peaceful scientific expedition. I understand they were studying a new variant of Ebola."

"Pretty convincing, right?"

Nikolai nodded, jaw muscles bunching as he chewed on what he'd seen.

"Yeah, very convincing."

"Yes. It was indeed an expedition of virologists and microbi-ologists from Yale University and two virologists seconded by the CDC. But they weren't attacked by soldiers of the PLA. Here."

With the track pad, Riley froze the video and brought up a detail of a soldier holding his weapon. An assault rifle. Even magnified, the resolution was still remarkable. She looked at them. "What do you see, Nikolai?"

Nikolai exchanged glances with Black. This was clearly a test. He carefully studied the screen shot. "Ah, okay. On that screen are three PLA soldiers plus a captain. Four scientists. and a fifth one on the ground who looks dead." He didn't know what else to say and looked at Black. "Right?" Black nodded with an enigmatic smile and Nikolai continued. "The soldiers are carrying QBZ-191s. They have body armor. One of them is carrying a grenade launcher, which is overkill for an encampment of scientists."

Riley turned to Pierce. "You saw the whole thing. Did anyone use a grenade launcher? Or hand grenades?"

"No. Just guns. And knives."

Yeah, Pierce had watched as a Chinese soldier had slit the throat of one scientist from behind, and gutted another. The scientists had been unarmed and dressed in tropical gear, some in lab coats.

"I give up. So, what are we missing, Riley?" Nikolai asked after a period of silence.

"Look more closely at the hand holding the rifle," she said quietly.

He checked. "Goddamn." Nikolai shook his head. "Missed it."

"Don't worry. I did, too," Black said. "The hand holding the rifle has six fingers. The other hand has six, too."

"It's a minor defect in deepfake software." Riley tapped the screen with a pen. "It can't replicate hands well, because the library of images it draws from is focused on faces and torsos and not hands. In a year or two, the system will have improved. As a matter of fact, in a year or two, deepfakes will be indistinguishable from the real thing and we'll all be in a ton of trouble."

Pierce and Black and Nikolai nodded. Pierce couldn't even imagine a world where you couldn't distinguish real from fake. It would be hell.

"So this crossed my desk and I immediately realized that it was a deepfake. We had a stroke of luck because it was released in-house a little early. Someone made a mistake. This is what I first saw. I'm sure the version released to the public is perfect. Creating a deepfake is an iterative process, each step better than the one before. Since I had the raw file, I tried stripping it."

She tapped on a few keys, and Pierce watched on in awe as the video went backward and forward in time, each time looking different. It was eerie. The faces were stripped of their features, tiny dots on the foreheads, cheeks, noses, chins, and lines between them, changing shape. Their clothes changed. Riley speeded it up until they had an entirely different video on the screen.

"Holy. Shit." Nikolai shook his head. Because what was on the screen were Western-looking faces on the operatives, wearing a distinctive unform they were all very familiar with.

He exchanged a startled look with Black.

"Sommers Group," Nikolai said. "This is serious stuff."

It was.

Operators of an American security company slaughtering American scientists. Nothing worse.

"They tried to recruit me," Pierce said, then clamped his jaw closed. He'd never told anyone, not even his best friend Raul Martinez.

Black side-eyed him. "Adrian Sommers?"

Pierce regretted having said anything. He looked down at the carpet. "Yeah."

"Son of a bitch." Black's face tightened. "He thought you were one of them. Fucker." Black turned to Riley. "Sorry."

"Well, from what I've seen of the company, Adrian Sommers is indeed a fucker," she said.

"Pierce here did an extremely brave thing, a truly honorable thing." Black was looking at Riley as if daring her to contradict him.

Riley looked at Pierce. Her eyes, this unearthly pale blue, seemed to look straight into him. "Emma told me what you and Raul did. It was incredibly brave. I don't know if I would have had the courage."

Yeah, it had taken balls. They bucked the entire military apparatus to report the guy, who got a hard-on from killing civilians on mission. Particularly female civilians. Particularly pregnant female civilians.

In any other circumstance, they would have had to face headwinds, but would have prevailed, because one of the scenes was secretly filmed. But their fuckhead commander's uncle was the head of the Armed Services Committee and they were threatened with court martial and Leavenworth.

There had been a minor revolt among their fellow SEALs, and the compromise was that they'd be allowed to leave the service quietly with an 'other than honorable' discharge. The one people got when caught with drugs. John Huntington and Douglas Kowalski, the heads of Alpha Security International, one of the best security firms in the country, had been waiting at the gates as they left their base for the last time.

"I wanted the two of you," Black said and gave a wintry smile. "But your buddies all worked at ASI, and Midnight said back off, so I had to step back."

"But working for the Sommers Group..." Riley's voice tapered off.

"Was out of the question," Pierce said harshly. Particularly now that he saw what they were capable of. And particularly now that he knew they had threatened Riley's life.

"The company is made up almost exclusively of men who rang the bell," Black said.

"Sorry? Is that a metaphor?" Riley asked, frowning.

"No," Black answered. "It's quite literal. Every SEAL who ever was has had to go through Hell Week, and it's called that for a reason. It's brutal. If you can't make it, for whatever reason, you ring a bell that is positioned right on the grinder, this concrete area where the candidates do their workouts. The workouts were hard, and the bell was right there. Sommers recruited from the men who rang the bell."

"Who quit," Riley said. She got it.

"Yeah. They have decent skills, most of them almost made the grade, but didn't. So Adrian Sommers thinks he's found a magic formula. Getting men who almost made it as SEALs, but didn't. But who still have skills."

"But, presumably, work cheaply."

"There you go. And they are fanatically loyal to Sommers because he pretends they are the real deal. And Sommers cuts corners and doesn't turn any work down because of pesky illegalities. He'll do anything if the price is right. Works mainly abroad, where there's not much he won't do."

Riley pointed to the screen. "Clearly."

The final stripping away of the layers that made up the deep fake showed Sommers operators gunning down American scientists with incredible ferocity. The Sommers Group logo was clearly visible on all the operators.

Nikolai couldn't take his eyes off the screen. "That's a degree of ferocity that's uncalled for. They look out of control. This was a slaughter, not a pitched battle to the death. And they were fighting unarmed scientists, anyway. They look ... deranged."

"Or hopped up on something," Riley mused.

"Some incredible stimulant." Pierce was thinking it through. "Some drug. Something powerful."

"There's something else," Riley said. Black cocked his head.

Pierce was amazed at how Black reacted to Riley.

Black was immensely powerful. He spoke to heads of state and they listened. He had an overwhelming command presence and intimidated most people. But he was leaning forward, completely open to what she was going to say.

He didn't intimidate Riley. She looked calm and serene.

It was Pierce who had problems with her. He was here to protect her. He'd been on close protection duty before and should have slipped right into bodyguard mode. Bodyguard mode was intense focus, 24/7, allowing for no distractions at all. Even a second's lack of attention could prove fatal. This was a young woman with important intel and dangerous enemies. A ruthless security company full of guys with guns perfectly willing to use them. Not to mention law enforcement. So he had to be fully focused.

Not constantly distracted by her beauty.

Damn. She was possibly the most beautiful woman he'd ever seen. He knew she was attractive. The IT department back at ASI had corkboards with photos of the four of them – Felicity, Hope, Emma and Riley—from their days at the NSA. Felicity, Hope and Emma were attractive women but *man*, Riley really stood out, as if the photo was in 3D for her. But in person? She was like walking hormones, reaching out to grab him by the balls. Without doing anything overt. No coy glances, no flipping her hair, no side-eyes to see what effect she was having on three alpha males.

Nope. She was all business.

This thing he was feeling, this massive distraction, was all on him. He was usually all business too, professionally. He was never distracted, and yet, here he was. Wondering what that perfect ivory skin felt like, what that lithe, slender body would feel like in his arms. What...

"Okay," Riley said and for a second, crazy in his own head, Pierce was ready to stand up and go to her because she'd said okay. As if she'd heard the insanity in his head and agreed to what he was thinking.

Sex.

Right now.

He tensed to stand up, when Riley said, "You both know how the NSO works, correct?"

And he untensed and sat back. Black looked at him, then back at Riley. But that look was enough to quell Pierce. He was here for a job, not to drool over a woman. No matter how pretty she was.

"I think we've got a handle on it," Black said, and Riley nodded.

"Yeah," Nikolai said.

"The NSO has 248 satellites."

They blinked. A sign of utter astonishment from three former SEALs.

"I thought—" Black began, and she smiled.

"Yeah, you thought there were something like thirty?"

He nodded.

"Nope. A lot of them are stealth and don't show up on radar. But that's not the point. The point is that the NSO basically covers the earth, and the photos the NSO shows the public are deliberately slightly out of focus. We've made great strides and our photos allow you to read a newspaper at 35,000 miles. And like I said, they cover most of the earth. We all are assigned various areas, and for a long while I was assigned the Chinese military, particularly the PLA on maneuvers. I studied them so carefully that I got to know some of the major players. This, for example, is Captain Chao Feng."

A face showed on her screen. Pierce glanced at Black. "Isn't that—"

"You have a good eye." Riley split the screen and showed the image that was making the rounds of the world press. Chinese soldiers mowing down American scientists, one officer screaming at the sky. He had a distinct face, very broad, with a scar near his eye. Captain Chao Feng. "Captain Chao happened to be in Sichuan province when the attack took place. We have dated video proving this. So whoever did this, made the deep-faked video, took facial maps of Chinese soldiers, and we have a million images of them, and transposed them on to the Sommers Group soldiers. But the thing is, the million images of them are all in-house. Inside the NSO. I don't think there is any other photo or video archive as rich in images of Chinese soldiers than the one the NSO has. So, much as I hate to think it, I suspect that the person or persons who made the deepfakes had access to the NSO archives."

"Or worked at the NSO." Pierce drew the obvious conclusion.

"Or worked at the NSO." Riley's voice was sad. "I hate that thought, but what can I say? It's inevitable. It was someone who had access to the archives, or worked at the NSO and who was very good. And it wasn't me."

"I imagine that the traces of whoever accessed the archives are long gone."

"If it was someone who was good enough to create these deepfakes, they were good enough to cover their traces, yeah. I hate that thought. NSO officers are nerdy and weird, but harm-less and loyal. Or so I thought." She sighed. "I also have no idea at all why the Chinese aren't publicizing the absence of Captain Chao from Africa."

"It suits them," Black said. "This happened at a moment in which hawks have the upper hand in the State Council, and President Liu is weak. They are going to push boundaries, see how far they can go. If it gets dangerous, and escapes their control, they can always back down, prove he wasn't there."

"China wants to see if they can blackmail us and then overrun Taiwan," Riley said.

Silence. It was true. Pierce realized how dangerous the situation was, how easily it could get out of hand. And how very easily these huge forces could crush this beautiful woman.

"I know some people in the Pentagon," Black said. Which was an understatement. He was very well-known in the Pentagon. And the White House. And Congress. "I'll take this to them and stop this. And see that Sommers is brought to justice. That massacre is horrific. And trying to get a war going as a cover-up, like he did, is treason. They'll throw the book at him."

"Not yet." Riley held up a finger and Black, who was halfway to his feet, sat back down again. Once again, Pierce was struck by Riley's self-possession. "What I showed you is not completely corroborated. I'm going to need my software and I'm going to need the version stored on my computer."

Pierce frowned. On her computer? She'd carried nothing with her other than a small purse. He had a bad feeling about this. "So where's your computer?"

"In my apartment. We need to go get it, now."

Pierce and Black and Nikolai spoke at the exact same moment.

"Absolutely not."

"Don't even think it."

"No way in hell."

5

It was almost comical. If it wasn't so awful, so very dangerous, she'd have laughed. Three grown men, three men used to command, speaking in unison. Black and Nikolai spoke in a low, even tone. Pierce growled.

But there was no way around this.

She sat patiently while the three of them told her she was crazy and then told her in detail exactly how crazy. Operators from the Sommers group were undoubtedly staking out her apartment. Even moving from the safe house was insane. Did she have a death wish? Did she even realize what she was asking?

Riley sat, barely listening, while they unspooled their thoughts, then waited until they both wound down. Jacob Black in particular looked astonished and vexed at the same time. He was clearly used to being obeyed instantly. When he'd finished his reasoning, he sat back, sure that he'd made his point.

Pierce, however, was more emotional. His voice was raw, hoarse. His jaws clenched and there was a line of perspiration along his hairline. "Do you remember that a couple of hours ago you nearly died at the hands of Sommers Group assholes? They were shooting at you, and it was a miracle I managed to arrive in time. Something really bad is happening and we need you to stop it. If something happens to you, the bad guys win. Is that what you want? For them to win because you want your own laptop?"

She understood where they were coming from, so she didn't snap back. Jacob Black was used to being obeyed, instantly, and Pierce and Nikolai, as former SEALs, were probably used to getting their own way, a lot.

They were also, all three, big men. Big and tall and strong. No one ever tried to bully them or intimidate them. It was the way of the world. Very few people told big, strong men what to do.

But she also wasn't used to being told what to do. No help had ever been forthcoming from her family. Her mother had been too wrapped up in the smoky craziness in her head, and her father had had no desire to be involved. So she'd made her own way in the world. Luckily, she was smart, had inherited some money from her grandmother, had sailed through three colleges with full rides, and had been recruited for good jobs before even graduating. The only road block had been the Boss from Hell at the NSA, but she'd had Felicity, Hope and Emma.

But this wasn't about her being difficult or making a point of not obeying. It was something else.

Riley sat up straight and looked at each of them in the eyes.

"I know you disapprove, all three of you, but I really need my computer and I am the one who has to get it. With all due respect," she touched the laptop Pierce had provided, "this is like the stone age club in *A Space Odyssey*. More or less as effective. My laptop has two programs that, no, are not in the cloud but even if they were, I couldn't download to this." She flicked her finger against the cover. "I worked on uncovering the deepfake at home, on my laptop, on my own time, because I wasn't sure of what I was seeing, but the fact is, proper proof is there and only there. Otherwise what we have is an improbable story and that's it. Not only that … I have a fail-safe security system, which requires my thumb print and no, I am not going to cut off my own thumb and give it to you. This is the only way we'll get solid proof. With my laptop. Which is in my apartment."

"Proper proof won't help you if you're dead!" Pierce said heatedly.

Riley took in a deep breath to respond, then Jacob Black chimed in. "Riley," he said in his deep, grave voice. "If anything happens to you, we cannot do anything. I understand you need your laptop. God knows I hate going on a mission without proper gear. We all do. But essentially, it's not what's on your laptop that's going to convince everyone. It's what is in your head. I think I can safely say that neither Pierce nor Nikolai nor I understand one tenth of what is necessary to prove that that video is a deepfake. Without you, we don't stand a chance."

"Can you send a drone?"

"Excuse me?"

"Can you send a silent drone to my house? To see the situation? We'll talk when we know what's going on."

Black exchanged a glance with Nikolai. "Sure," he said. He consulted his cell. "As a matter of fact, there's a drone of ours not five minutes from where you live." He held up a finger when he saw her outraged expression. "It's not what you think. When I got a message from ASI and from Pierce, your address was included in the package of data. SOP."

She subsided. It probably was SOP and not him checking her background.

"There," he said, having sent a message. "The drone will be there soon."

"Does it have IR capability?"

"Yeah."

"Ok, let's use these minutes." She gave a little 5-minute seminar on imaging tech, but could see that all three of them looked relieved when a soft chime sounded from Black's phone.

"Send it to the monitor on the wall," she suggested, and the big screen on the wall lit up, showing the familiar scenes from her neighborhood. She didn't know Washington, DC well, because since she'd gotten the job at NSO, her life had been the job and home, home and the job. But she was a walker and a runner and knew her neighborhood intimately.

It was getting dark. People and animals were showing up more as heat images than regular images. But Riley could read the heat images perfectly.

She got out her laser pointer from her fanny pack, highlighting the areas she described.

"Okay, here's my place. It's a former mansion built in 1920, now divided up into six apartments. I'm on the third floor, here. Send the drone over the roof, please."

Black murmured something into his cell and the drone moved over the roof and she highlighted her apartment.

"This is mine, in the southeast corner. And I'll bet—" She turned to Jacob Black. "Can I have control over the drone?"

He looked startled, which she was sure didn't happen often. "Ahh, sure. But it's fairly complex. We have people in-house to run the drones. They've been specially trained."

Riley just looked at him. He sighed, texted, got an answer. "Okay, control passing to you ... now."

Riley studied the drone dashboard. Complex, but not too complex. And the drone had real capabilities. Good.

She swooped around, familiarizing herself with the controls. Good feedback, and the drone was steady. She brought it to the front of her house and sure enough, there they were. Two men in an SUV, just sitting there. Switching to IR, she saw it was just the two men, no one else.

"And, gentlemen, here's our surveillance team."

Jacob Black was on the phone, quietly giving someone the license plate number to check.

The driver buzzed down his window and stuck his head out for a moment. Pierce got up and moved close to the monitor, then swore. "Goddamn."

Riley put a hand on his shoulder. "You know them?"

"Yeah." She could feel him almost vibrating under her hand. "Him. The driver. Son of a bitch got a recruit killed during Hell Week. Knocked a teammate off course to get ahead and the man fell and hit his head on a rock. The trainers only found out by accident because it showed up in footage. Some guy was making a documentary about SEAL training. His name is Harry Dutton."

Jacob Black heard and looked more carefully at the monitor. "Son of a bitch is right. And he's with the right company, the Sommers Group. Staking out the apartment of a young woman. About his speed."

They were focusing really hard on this guy, which she understood. But they needed to focus on her getting her computer.

Riley coughed and the three men swiveled their heads. "About me getting my laptop ..."

"No," Jacob Black said.

"Not advised," Nikolai said.

"No way in hell," Pierce specified.

"I need—"

"What part of two operators staking out your house do you not understand?" Pierce tried to make his voice reasonable but the stress came through. His voice cracked.

Riley sent the drone around the perimeter of the house. "Do you guys see anyone else?"

Pierce shook his head. "No. So?"

"So ..." She circled the perimeter of her house with the laser pointer. She lived in a leafy part of Alexandria. "If we park the car here, two blocks away and one block down, we can come to my building via back lots. There are no dogs along this route and we would be invisible to the two guys staking out my building."

She traced a path from where they'd park the car to the side of her building.

Pierce cocked his head. "They cover the front entrance. How do you get into the building?"

This was tricky. She had to tell a ... not truth. She was terrible at lying, truly awful. Usually her voice changed pitch, and shook. But she had to remind herself she needed her laptop to get out of the mess she was in, and there was only one path forward.

"Can't see it because shrubbery is in the way, but there's an entrance to the basement, leading to service stairs. There's only one security camera, at the entrance, and I can keep that going. I'd be in and out in five minutes."

"Great." Jacob Black clapped his hands and stood. "Either Pierce or I will go. Nikolai has to head back to the office to arrange logistics for tomorrow. You wait in the car with whoever isn't going."

"Ah..." Riley took a big breath. "That's not going to work. I added to the security at the door to my apartment. It requires my thumbprint. Sorry. Again, not willing to have my thumb cut off like in the movies. It's going to have to be me going up. I swear, I'll be fast. In and out, and then we come back here and I'll show you the underlying structure of the deepfake. Mr. Black—uh, Jacob, you're not going to be able to convince anyone until I can break it down. This whole thing has got a momentum of its own. The Seventh Fleet is sailing to the Taiwan Strait. Right now."

That put them over the edge. She could feel it in the room.

Usually, Riley was better with data than with people, but even she could feel when something was right. She'd kept an eye on the chyrons of the news feeds and they were more dire by the hour.

Riley glanced outside the window at the gathering dark. It would take about twenty minutes to get to her place. It would be full dark by the time they got there. Great. She could navigate her apartment blindfolded, wouldn't need any light, not even a flashlight.

She stood, quivering with tension, ready to *gogogo*. With her laptop, she could prove her innocence, prove that the US might be going to war on a lie. Without it, she was just sinking into quicksand, deeper by the minute. "Are we going or not?"

Pierce stood too, on a sigh. "One thing has to be made clear. Black and I are the security experts. If we feel something is wrong, we all pull out. If there's even a hint of something wrong, we all pull out. And you commit to obeying us instantly. We clear on that?"

"Oh yes." Yeah, security was their jam. Hers was intel. If they felt there was danger they couldn't deal with, they were all leaving. No problem.

Except—she would be left with the situation as it was. Her life in ruins, with the police and an ethically challenged security company made up of trained killers after her. She needed her laptop. She needed to make Pierce and Jacob Black *understand*, not just agree because they liked her, but *understand* how she was telling the truth, and understand how very dangerous the truth was.

And understand enough to explain it in terms a ten-year-old could understand.

They trooped out, Nikolai heading back to the Black Inc. office near Dupont Circle and the three of them to her apartment.

Black gave the wheel to Pierce, which sort of surprised her. Black seemed like the kind of guy who'd always take the wheel. But then she'd seen Pierce's driving ability and didn't doubt that if they were somehow spotted and chased, he'd manage. It spoke to Black's intelligence that he didn't pull rank and sit in the driver's seat, just automatically rode shotgun.

Riley got in right behind Pierce. It wasn't until they were halfway there that she admitted to herself it was so she could watch him without anyone noticing.

She was insanely stressed. Otherwise how to explain this fascination with watching him drive, even from the back? Everything she could see was a real treat. He had big, strong, very elegant hands and she stared at his right hand on the knob of the stick shift as he played it like a musical instrument. The ride was incredibly smooth, even in DC traffic, which was like the 7th Circle of Hell.

Not only his hand was fascinating. He'd rolled up his sleeves and his right forearm was riveting, too. Strong, lean muscles in play every time he switched gears. His shoulders were so broad they exceeded the width of the car seat, so she could watch that, too. Shiny, blue-black hair that shifted when he turned briefly to talk to Black. They were carrying on an intense discussion which she couldn't quite make out, though she could distinguish the tones. Black's voice was deep and rough, Pierce's voice was just as deep but smoother. Every once in a while, she could catch a word, a phrase. Lines of sight. Shooting angle. Range. Drone.

She had a few ideas about this last thing, but that was for later.

Not being able to participate in their discussion, she fell into her own head and analyzed her situation. That was what she was good at. Analysis. Not action. But there was only so much to analyze beyond the fact that she was in the shit, so she simply sat back and watched the landscape, not taking anything in, not thinking at all.

A form of meditation.

Finally, Pierce pulled smoothly into a parking slot, on the street they'd agreed on, and killed the engine. The vehicle was so sound-proofed she couldn't even hear the ticking of a cooling engine.

Riley stuck her head between the seats. "Can you give me the drone flight controller?"

"Sure," Black answered, and handed her a ruggedized monitor, clearly meant for the battlespace.

"Okay. I'll show you where we're going." She tracked a path through back yards and along alleyways to the side of her building. "If we stick to this path, there are no security cameras. And there are none on the side of my building."

The men nodded.

"I imagine the drone can't pick up audio, correct?"

Jacob Black sighed.

"As a side project, Hope and I are designing a sound sensor unit for drones that can be activated remotely. A simple add-on."

"I'd buy that in a heartbeat," Black answered immediately. "For whatever price you asked."

"No price." She looked at him, at that hard, authoritative face. "You can have it for free, as long as ASI can have it, too. I am very grateful for the help you and your company are providing. ASI, too. It would be an honor to let you have it."

Black dipped his head, like a king accepting a tribute.

"Okay, your drone needs to hover without moving at all, close to the car with the two operators."

Pierce frowned. "That would be hard since we won't be able to guide it while running through backyards." Black nodded his head.

It always amazed Riley that men never ran through their devices thoroughly.

"Here." She took a lot of care not to sound condescending. She knew this stuff because basically she didn't have a life. They were outward-directed and moved around in meatspace. She was inner-directed and lived inside her head and inside her devices. She found the almost hidden setting to stabilize the drone—who designed these things anyway?—showed it to them, then got out of the vehicle. She was quivering to get started.

The two men were still in the car, doors open, staring down at the monitor, slack-jawed.

"How did you—" Pierce began, but she interrupted.

"Come *on.*"

They exchanged a glance and got out. Now that she was close to her apartment and her computer, she was in a fever of impatience. The two men seemed to be moving in slow motion. They were freaking SEALs and were supposed to be almost supermen. Superpowers included speed, right?

She didn't say anything as Pierce hauled some stuff out from the back of the SUV. A backpack and three combat vests. He wouldn't budge until she put one on.

It was huge, almost twice the size of her chest and cut into her thighs. Riley hated it, but she didn't say anything about it. One thing she had to say to them, though, was how to behave.

"We're going to be moving through backyards. Though we'll be hidden by shrubbery most of the time, if you could hide your weaponry, that would be great. It's one thing to look out the window and see two huge scary guys, and quite another to look out the window and see two huge scary guys with guns. Even if you're with me and I'm not huge and scary. Okay, come on."

They were so slow. She just took off, which was the only way to get them to *move.* Pierce gave an outraged huff of breath and followed. She didn't look back to see if Jacob Black was with them but she was sure he was.

At least they were quiet. Amazingly quiet, considering they went through hedges and shrubbery and considering how large they were. You wouldn't know they were there.

Riley knew this area very well, knew where to go and how, but once they actually got going, they had no difficulty in keeping up.

Finally, she unlatched a gate covered in ivy that was more or less invisible, and there they were—on the left side of her building. Her apartment was three stories up. She could see the wrought-iron balcony and dark windows. In there was her computer and she longed for it. It would straighten everything out and the nightmare would be over.

Riley gestured to see the monitor and Pierce handed it over. Just as she hoped. The two operators were still in their SUV, waiting for her to walk through the front door of her building like a moron.

Well, good luck waiting for that.

She was going to get her freedom, and vindication. Revenge for Henry's death, too.

The combat vest fell to the ground with a thud.

She jumped.

6

S*on of a bitch!* Pierce had just enough presence of mind not to shout it out loud, just in his head. He couldn't believe his eyes. He thought Riley would go through this basement entrance—which he'd just realized was non-existent—and then she took a running leap at the side of the building.

For a moment, it looked like magic. Like those movies where a character with super powers like Spiderman just walks up the side of a building. Then he realized it was a wall climb for her. She used every single handhold and foothold to make it to each floor's small balcony. Pulling herself up to the second-floor balcony via the spout, she stood on the top of the railing, pushed off—his breath snagged and he moved forward instinctively to catch her before realizing she didn't need catching. She caught the bottom railing on the third-floor balcony, pulled herself up, launched herself up to stand on the balcony.

And disappeared.

Pierce looked at Jacob Black, not daring to say a word. But Black looked as stunned as he was. Sooner than he thought possible, Riley reappeared on the balcony with gloves on, a backpack and a length of rope looped over her shoulder. She did a complicated flip down to the balcony below, quickly knotted the rope around the far end post and slid down to alight noiselessly and easily on the ground.

Beginning to end, maybe five minutes. Done as smoothly as any SEAL could have done it. More easily, even, because she was very light.

Without saying a word, Riley made off in the direction they'd come from, stopped and looked back.

They were observing sound discipline and no one could speak, but her expression was clear. *Come on, guys!* Riley glanced at the monitor velcroed to Black's combat vest and he checked and nodded. The team on the stake out was still there. Hadn't moved.

Pierce picked up her combat vest which clearly she wasn't going to wear, and they all hurried back to where they'd left their vehicle. Soon Pierce pulled out.

Riley had opened her backpack and extracted the laptop. Pierce didn't turn around, but he did see Black open his eyes a little, the SEAL equivalent of pure astonishment, as he looked at the laptop. All the IT brainiacs back in Portland had one—a computer that seemed to have been transported from the future, or given to them by an alien civilization, in slight variations of matte, non-reflective colors. No brands. There was someone in Tokyo who specialized in leading-edge computing and he had a number of beta users, including Felicity, Hope, Emma and apparently, Riley.

"Does this vehicle have wifi?" she asked. "I don't want to use my hotspot. It might be traced."

"Sure." Black took out a visiting card, wrote something on the back and turned around in his seat and handed it to her. "Here's the password."

Riley smiled. It was blinding. Pierce was watching her in the rear-view mirror and nearly had a heart attack. Smiles like that should be illegal. Even Black was a little taken aback.

Black had never been seen with a woman by his side and seemed perennially single. There were rumors about a girl in his past, a lost love, but no one really knew the story. He was always all business around women, but even he was affected by that smile.

That smile was fucking magic.

Pierce tightened his grip on the steering wheel, telling himself sternly to get his head out of his ass. She wasn't paying him any attention, anyway, head bent over her computer. The one she'd risked her life to get.

Riley stayed glued to her computer all the way back to the safe house. Pierce could have turned the GPS on, but didn't. He had a superb sense of direction. Once he'd gone a route, he remembered it.

Nobody spoke. There was a lot to talk about with Black, but without Riley's input, they'd just be talking in circles. And she was immersed in her own stuff. If they batted ideas about, they'd just be disturbing her, and they wouldn't be good ideas anyway, since they had incomplete intel.

On the road, Pierce tried to piece together what he knew. There were discrete points. Someone had killed Riley's boss, most likely operators from the Sommers Group, because Riley had given Henry Yu intel, which he sent to his own boss. Pierce had no idea who that was. It was possible Henry Yu's boss was a mole, or at least in the pay of the Sommers Group and told Adrian Sommers. Once they'd killed Yu, they went after Riley because they understood she was the source of the information.

She alone knew that the video roiling foreign affairs, leading to a possible confrontation with the People's Republic of China, if not to armed conflict, was a deepfake. A really good one. He had no idea who had created the deepfake.

The deepfake was incredibly dangerous and Riley held the key.

That was more or less all he knew, and trying to piece it all together into a coherent picture was giving him a headache.

Plus, he was trying to run through what he knew while a good chunk of his brain was taken up with this wild attraction. An attraction stronger than any he'd ever felt before, to a woman who wasn't showing any signs of attraction back.

Which was ... hard.

Pierce didn't sleep around. He didn't like impersonal sex. SEAL groupies in bars left him cold. Plus he'd been deployed under cover for a year and knew having sex with a woman would be painting a target on her back. However, in the past, when he was attracted, he'd been lucky because the woman in question was attracted right back.

So it all worked out okay. He didn't hurt for sex, but it didn't rule his life. He was in charge of his dick, not the other way around.

He was wildly attracted to Riley—had been since he first saw her picture back in Portland. But now he had a personality to add to the picture, and he liked it all. She was the most beautiful woman he'd ever seen, which was saying a lot because the IT department back in Portland was made up of Riley's friends, who were all unusually good-looking.

Not as good-looking as Riley, but that would be hard.

She was also fascinating. Incredibly smart, brave and resourceful. And she could climb a building like Spiderman. There was that.

But Pierce tucked away his fascination, because right now the first priority was keeping this woman safe. She had real enemies and now had the police after her. The Sommers group had a lot of money, and cops earned very little. If Riley were ever arrested, he had no doubt she'd be whacked while in custody.

Not going to happen.

"Riley," he said quietly. The soft sound of keyboard strokes continued. "Riley," he said, a little less quietly.

Her head came up, eyes a little unfocused.

"We're here."

"Oh!" Her eyes widened and she looked around, orienting herself. Something warriors never had to do. They were always oriented because the price for losing yourself in your head could be death. And not usually a pleasant one.

But Riley, like her friends back in Portland, could get lost in her head, at the drop of a hat. They dealt in abstracts: algorithms, patterns, pixels. Pierce and his teammates dealt in blood and bone and steel.

They didn't lose themselves in their head because that was a good way to get it chopped off. Two teammates had been beheaded in the 'Stan.

"Sorry." In an instant Riley stowed the laptop in the backpack and was ready.

"Nothing to be sorry about," Black rumbled.

Pierce was at her door, offering his hand. Which was insane. He'd just watched her do something that required lithe athleticism and superb balance. She could make it to the ground from a vehicle on her own just fine.

But it was habit and ... well, he wanted to touch her. And she accepted his hand because the SUV was high off the ground. She put her hand in his and he held it as she descended like a ballerina, feet pointed to the ground.

He held her hand a second longer than necessary, and she left her hand in his. Their eyes met and he couldn't have looked away if you had pointed a gun at his head.

Her eyes were like some cosmic black hole, only light blue instead of black. They absorbed all the light... the rest of the world became dark. You just fell into them, shiny, silver, with a rim of dark blue.

Whoa.

Black was looking at them over the top of the vehicle. His face was absolutely expressionless, betraying nothing. But an operator in the middle of a crisis losing himself in a protectee's eyes ... not good.

Pierce dropped her hand and followed her into the safe house.

They sat as they had before, Riley at one end of the small couch, Pierce beside her, Black in an armchair.

Riley opened up her laptop and Pierce nearly fell into that, too. She didn't have the program Hope and Emma had, where you could see the screen only head-on, invisible to anyone to the side. Pierce could see just fine.

The screen had colors more vivid than any he'd ever seen, floating and morphing in an abstract pattern that was hypnotic. You couldn't tear your eyes away from it. If he had that on his computer, he'd never get any work done.

Riley opened a program and her fingers floated over the keyboard, barely exerting pressure, blindingly fast. It must have been an intuitive keyboard and had to use some version of AI, it was that fast.

Riley looked at him, then at Black. "Okay, I am going to show you a program I wrote which is going to be more useful than I ever imagined. It peels back deepfakes fast. I wrote it on a dare."

"Black Inc. will buy it from you," Black said instantly. He saw, like Pierce, the massive utility of a program like that, in a future that would be full of deepfakes.

"No," Riley said, peering into the screen, navigating her way to somewhere. "I told you before, I'll gladly give it to you and to ASI. And I'll train your people if you like. If I ever get out from under this massive weight." She stopped navigating and lifted her hands. "I am also going to show you images taken from the NSO database, which is absolutely illegal. I shouldn't have them and I am subject to instant termination of service if discovered, and on top of that, I have broken a dozen federal laws." She gave a harsh laugh that morphed into a sob, stifled by a hand over her mouth. She coughed, took a moment, began again. "Though frankly, that is nothing compared to the trouble I am currently in."

Riley looked so miserable Pierce reached out to touch her hand. He couldn't help himself, and didn't give a shit that Black saw. It was unprofessional, but he didn't work for Black, and could do whatever the fuck he wanted.

But Black didn't look disapproving. If anything, he looked a little sad, which was weird on that tough face.

"Sorry," Riley said, shaking her head and sitting up straighter.

"Told you there was no need to apologize." Black smiled. Black, smiling. It was really rare. It looked like it hurt.

"Anyway, when I saw the video, which was making the rounds of people working in national security, I immediately recognized it as one of ours, from one of our satellites. Identifying it as NSO satellite footage is complex and highly technical. I can run through it if you like, but can you take my word for it? Speed things up?"

"Absolutely," Pierce said. Felicity, Hope and Emma had always maintained that Riley was perhaps the best of them. That was more than good enough for him.

"Yes," Black said.

Riley blew out a breath. "Good. So, the first time I saw the video there were some anomalies, like the six fingered hands I showed you. I saw two more iterations crop up in the space of a couple of hours and each iteration was better than the last. Like I said, that is how deep fakes are created – they are GANned.

Generative Adversarial Network. The system goes back and forth, eliminating anomalies, making the image better and better. My program does the opposite—it strips the image of the improvements and takes it back to the original."

She worked the keyboard, then sat back. "Look."

Pierce and Black leaned forward. It was exactly as Riley had said. Her program stripped the image, over and over, until the Chinese soldiers disappeared and Sommers Group soldiers appeared.

"Here is where it gets interesting." Riley was manipulating the video. "So you know AI can invent people who look very plausible? You've all seen those articles with photos of ordinary-looking people, who are all invented by AI?"

Yeah. Pierce had seen them and thought it was creepy. He nodded and Black did too.

"Well, here's the thing. AI can make those faces up because it references literally millions of photos. But there aren't *that* many photos of Chinese faces available, so they were stumped. But as I told you earlier, you know who has a huge database of Chinese faces? We do! The NSO. And it just so happens that for the past year I have been assigned the China desk, which is what it would be if we were CIA. Actually, what I do is study shots and videos taken over mainland China and over equatorial Africa where the Chinese are very active, and flag things of interest. Here, let me show you."

Her fingers blurred over the keyboard. The monitor split into two. On the right-hand side was a freeze frame of the Chinese soldiers marauding. One by one, their faces were high-lighted and brought up as a close up. On the other side of the screen, were the same faces, only normal. Not screaming, not attacking. One at parade rest, one getting into an off-road vehi-cle, one practicing at a gun range. All normal scenes of soldiers' lives.

"What you see are the Chinese faces their AI were able to use. And since these images are top secret, the inescapable conclusion I came to is that the whole GAN, everything, was done in-house, at the NSO. I can hack and try to find out who there did the deepfake video—if it was someone in-house, he or she would know how to cover their tracks. Whoever it is did it for a lot of money, obviously," she added bitterly.

"Lot of people will do a lot of bad stuff for money, and Adrian Sommers is rolling in it," Black said. "He can buy just about anyone."

Pierce knew he was right. Black himself would never white-wash a video showing a massacre, and Pierce knew that he and his teammates back at ASI would never be tempted by any amount of money. Not a million dollars, not a billion dollars. He knew that because he'd been offered an obscene amount of money for covering up a murder. Murders. After he and Raul had watched their new commanding officer shoot up civilians in country. For sport.

When Pierce and Raul reported him, they knew it would be hard, but not how hard. Captain Fuckhead's uncle was a really powerful politician. Chairman of the Armed Forces Committee. Uncle Fuckhead had come down on them like a ton of bricks, threatening a court martial, dishonorable discharge, loss of pension, the works. Not before trying the easy way. Offering a cool five million each to withdraw the report.

He and Raul hadn't needed to consult with each other. They were both nauseated at the idea of being part of Captain Fuck-head getting away with murder.

But a lot of people had urged them to take the money and duck.

A lot of people would have been willing to take the money.

"Well, no one can buy *me*." Riley looked up. "So someone at NSO, which is charged with safeguarding the country's security from the skies, sold out. We might go to *war* over a lie to cover someone's ass."

Riley had white nostrils, lines bracketing her mouth. This idea affected her deeply, that a security agency harbored people who'd sell out their country.

It affected him, too. And Black. Though it wasn't a new idea to them, as it was to her.

"Here." Riley handed him and Black a piece of paper each, on which she had written a string of letters and numbers.

"What's this?" Pierce glanced at it. Long, random, impossible to memorize, which was probably the point.

"I just now set up a site in the darknet and I just gave you both the password. Without that password, no one will ever find it, so guard that password with everything you've got. Memorize it, if you can."

Pierce had a good memory, but he couldn't could trust his memory that much. If Riley said to memorize it, it meant that she had. But to her, and to her friends back at ASI, numbers were like friends.

He'd transcribe the password somewhere super safe and then destroy the slip of paper.

"Everything I just told you, every scrap of intel, my program, the NSO videos, my commentary, it's all on the site. Everything. Just in case—" her voice turned hoarse. She stopped for a moment, then cleared her throat. "Just in case something happens to me. Don't let them get away with this. They might be willing to lead us into Armageddon for a cover-up. So if anything happens, go after them with everything you've got."

The hell with what Black might think. Pierce picked up her hand. It was ice cold. "We will."

Her voice turned fierce, those light eyes glowing. "Promise me."

"Promise."

She turned to Black who nodded. "Promise."

Their promises carried weight. Pierce was at ease promising his own support and the backing of his company, which was strong and resourceful. Black's promise was powerful too. He would never promise something he wouldn't deliver, and his company was one of the biggest security companies in the world.

Tears shone in Riley's eyes. "Okay," she whispered. "Okay. Thank you. These people need to be brought down."

And suddenly, Pierce saw it. Riley was a warrior, just as much as he and Raul and his teammates were. As much as Black was. She wasn't trained to shoot and fight, but she had a warrior's heart. Her mouth was set, her eyes glowed with purpose. She had clearly taken into account as a possibility her own death. Just as Pierce did, and Raul and the others. You go into a mission willing to give it your all, aware that you might die. Accepting that.

Riley was fully aware of the forces arrayed against her, a wall of bad guys and the forces of law and order. Gunning for her.

On her side, ASI and Black Inc. But above all, her sense of right and wrong. And though she didn't have muscle power, she had formidable brain power and she was backed by her friends —three women who were the smartest people he knew.

Riley clearly felt this was her mission, and she was going to give it her all, and if that included her life, so be it.

However ...

Over his dead body.

Pierce sensed Black was moved by her words, too. Black wasn't attracted to her the way Pierce was, and he wasn't friends with her friends, though Emma had recently saved his life. But he could recognize courage and honor. Black was a patriot through and through, and understood the consequences of the Sommers group winning.

Including possible war with a super power.

They could count on Black to the bitter end.

Black stood. Riley craned her neck to look him in the face.

"Riley."

"Sir?"

"Jacob."

"Okay, Jacob."

"We're all going to do our very best to stop this. You've given us an amazing array of weapons, and I thank you. You've gathered these weapons at great cost to yourself. I know you must feel like you've lost everything—your job, your friend, everything in your life—but trust me when I say we'll move heaven and earth to make sure things work out for you."

She nodded, but looked like she didn't believe him.

"I'm going to start making some calls, and tomorrow we'll meet with the Crisis Group in the Pentagon. In the meantime, I'm stationing operators front *and* back, and they'll be scouting the perimeter on foot. You and Pierce will be as safe as possible here. On my way out, I'll have a good restaurant nearby send you some food. So have a nice meal and rest, both of you, because the next few days are going to be turbulent. Drink some wine, relax. You're safe."

"Yes, si—Yes, Jacob."

A slight smile crossed his austere face. "Do you like Italian?"

"Love it."

"Do you eat meat?"

"Absolutely."

The smile broadened. "Okay then. The food will be arriving shortly. Our guys outside will take delivery."

Clearly, Black wasn't thinking of him. Pierce could be a vegan teetotaler for all anyone cared. Fair enough. It was Riley who needed relaxation, good food, a good night's sleep. She was carrying too heavy a burden as it was.

Black was holding out a big hand to Riley, which she took gingerly. He shook her hand gently, briefly. "Riley. It was a pleasure meeting you. You've done something extraordinary for your country. I can't tell you how much I admire you. Tomorrow we're going to change history, and it will be thanks to you."

She flushed at the unexpected compliment. To have Jacob Black say he admired you was something else. Good. She'd been as pale as ice and it was great to see her with a little color in her cheeks.

"Pierce." Black gave him a look which was a summons and Pierce accompanied him to the door.

Black put a hand on his shoulder. "This is going to be hard," he said.

"Tell me something I don't know. But we do hard. We trained to do hard."

"Yeah, we do. Like I said, I'm going to set up some meetings tomorrow in the Pentagon and in Congress. Maybe the White House, if I can. Riley is going to have to come to most of those meetings. I hate that because it exposes her, but there's no other way."

Pierce hated it too. If it were up to him, he'd pack Riley in cotton, put her in the panic room of this super secure safe house, and wait it all out. Keep her safe. But a lot of non-tech people would have to be convinced, and she was the best person for that. No way could he or Black get up to speed enough to convince others.

"Sommers will do anything to get to her. He's dangerous."

"It's all dangerous. I can tell you right now that there's a substantial number of people in power, inside the military and out, who are salivating at the thought of a limited war with China. Nobody wants to go nuclear—though that can't be completely ruled out—but a nice little war, off in the China Sea, testing out new weapons systems, maybe securing the Taiwan

Strait—that would suit them just fine. And they'd have no desire to hear that the proof they've got of Chinese provocation is fake. Not to mention that the woman who proved that is wanted for questioning for murder."

"It's up to us to make sure Riley can testify."

"I'll make sure she gets to see the right people. You make sure she stays safe."

Pierce resisted the urge to salute. Neither of them was in the military, and anyway, Black wouldn't have been his commanding officer. But the urge was strong.

Black turned in the doorway and looked at Riley sitting on the couch. He lifted a long forefinger and raised his voice. "Oh, and Riley!" She cocked her head. "No climbing buildings!"

His face contorted strangely, and an odd sound came out of his chest. Laughter. The Jacob Black version of laughter. Luckily Riley recognized it immediately for what it was and smiled back.

Black turned back to him and patted his shoulder. "Okay, food should be arriving very soon. There'll be a little of everything, and some good wine. There are clean clothes in the bedroom. Women's clothes, too. Oh, and Pierce—"

"Yeah?"

They were at the open door. Across the street Pierce could see a stake-out car, and he knew there were others. He was thinking about rota systems and convoy configurations when Black leaned over and murmured directly into his ear.

"Condoms are in the top drawers of the bedside tables in the bedrooms."

7

B y the time Riley took another shower and rummaged through the surprisingly broad choice of women's clothing, food had arrived. She heard the front door open and male voices talking while she put on a sky-blue sweat suit and found a pair of slippers that fit her. There was a selection of footwear, too. Pumps to sneakers to sandals to boots, in a range of sizes. They were ready for anything and anybody.

God only knew what would be available to the men since she imagined more men used the safehouse than women. Except for her friends in the IT department, ASI was made up of all men, all—with one exception, Hope's guy Luke Reynolds—former SEALs. And the Black Inc. people she'd seen so far were all men.

She was used to working in an all-male environment, though the people working at NSO were men in the sense of having a Y chromosome, but that was it, compared to men like Pierce and Mr. Black. Jacob.

The guys she worked with were either underweight or overweight, had no muscle tone at all, and had faces that never saw the sun. They all looked like ghosts—pale and insubstantial.

Not Pierce.

Nope.

Again, when she entered the dining room, he stood. Which wasn't necessary but nice. He seemed to fill the room with his presence—tall, strong without being gym-rat muscly, at ease in his body. Most of the men she knew fidgeted, twitched, averted their eyes. Happiest alone at their desks with their computers and bag of Doritos.

Pierce kept his eyes right on her every step of the way. He circled the small table and held her chair out for her. Was that part of SEAL training?

The table almost groaned with food and he'd pulled over another table for the overrun. There seemed to be some of everything, in great abundance—two types of pasta, green and white; two types of red meat—ossobuco and tagliata; chicken *al mattone* with onion rings; a big mixed salad with lots of aromatic rocket; baked peppers; four bruschette with bright red cherry tomatoes. The other table was filled with fresh diced fruits, a big bowl of panna cotta, six cannoli, and—

Riley pointed. "Is that tiramisu?"

Pierce smiled, showing a dimple in his right cheek. Ack! So unfair. Overkill. "It is."

"My favorite," she sighed.

"Mine, too. But then everything here is my favorite. Black said he didn't try for fancy, but good, and he sure delivered."

"Man, he really did. There's enough food here for a platoon of SEALs, not just the two of us."

"There's also four croissants and berries for tomorrow morning."

Riley glanced at the kitchen. "I saw an espresso machine, so breakfast is going to be really nice. Is there fresh milk?"

"There is."

"He thought of everything."

"Well, considering you might be saving the free world, maybe even human civilization itself, I guess he thought it was worth it."

That wiped the smile off her face. For a second, seeing the amazing food, giving off even more amazing smells, in the company of the most attractive man she'd ever seen, had made her forget why they were there. It all came rushing back in.

"I'm sorry I said that. Don't think about it." Pierce covered her hand with his. It was warm and hard. "Let's eat and relax. There's nothing more we can do now. You've done everything you could. Now we're going to keep you safe and Black is going to try to convince his contacts at the Pentagon and in the Senate that it's all a fake. And you gave him all the ammo he'll need."

"My ammo won't stop people filled with malice and greed who have no desire to understand the truth."

"No." He stopped smiling. "We'll just have to hope that the sane people outnumber the greedy people, then."

Unfortunately, Riley wasn't too sure there were that many sane people around, untouched by greed.

But she quite literally could not change humanity right now. And a vast hunger had come roaring up from somewhere. She hadn't eaten since she'd gotten up this morning at six a.m. In the meantime. she'd uncovered a conspiracy, learned of her boss's death, been chased and shot at, and climbed the side of her house.

She took in a deep breath and started piling food onto her plate. Pierce was piling even more on his.

"You took steak, so can I pour you some red wine?"

She held up her stemmed glass. "You certainly can. What's the wine?"

He turned the bottle so he could read the label and his eyebrows shot up. "Whoa. Brunello di Montalcino 2022." He filled her glass.

"One of the best wines produced by Italy and that's saying a lot." She held the glass up to her nose and took in a deep sniff. It was heavenly, blending really well with the scent of the perfectly cooked meat, the rocket, and the peppers. Like some expensive perfume. Pierce filled his plate with pasta—tagliatelle with tomato sauce and melted mozzarella. He paused, fork in mid-air. "You're not eating the pasta?"

"I was trained to think strategically. If I eat the pasta, there'd be no room for the tiramisu."

He smiled at her, speared a forkful of tagliatelle and twisted it around the fork. "Smart lady. They told me you were smart, and they were right."

Her heart gave a sharp pang. 'They' were her friends—Felicity, Hope and Emma—and she missed them fiercely right now. She always missed them. The group they'd formed when they all worked at the NSA, even though it was in self-defense against the Boss from Hell, had been the happiest she'd ever been. The closest thing she'd ever had to a family. She'd loved it and she missed it.

Now, all three of her friends were working together across the country, in Portland, Oregon, and she was stuck on the other coast.

"How are they doing?"

"Mm?" Pierce was really enjoying his pasta. He swallowed and looked at her. "Who?"

"Felicity, Hope and Emma. How are they doing? I really miss them."

He put his fork down. "How are they doing? Well, let's see. Felicity is just about ready to pop, and it's a race to see whether the kids come out first or Metal has a stroke first."

"The kids. Twins." She sighed. Felicity had always been the super-efficient one. Two kids for the pain of one. "Though I understand it's been a hard pregnancy."

"Yeah. Hard on Metal, too. Felicity hasn't complained, not once, and has always done as much work as possible, though no one expected her to. It's Metal who complained. She barfed her way through the first three months, and even now, she'll throw up occasionally. Metal has lost ten years off his life."

"He'll be a good dad." Riley had never met Felicity's husband but, by all accounts, he loved Felicity and was looking forward to fatherhood when he wasn't overwhelmed by her morning, noon, afternoon and night sickness. Felicity loved him right back.

"Yeah, he will be a really good dad once he stops freaking."

"And Hope and Emma? How are they doing?"

"Just great. They both love it at ASI. It's a great company to work for. All three of them are appreciated and well treated. We're all like a family."

Yeah. That was the impression she'd got when they talked. That her friends were happy. A family ... what would that feel like? She'd never really had one. It must be great ...

"Eat," Pierce said firmly. "And drink. You've had a traumatic day."

She speared a bite of tagliata, and oh ... it melted in her mouth. "Tomorrow won't be better. Nor will the day after. And if there is a war that escalates, none of the tomorrows will be better."

"It won't come to that. You have a lot of firepower on your side. And we have to hope reason will prevail."

She sighed. "You're a Navy SEAL, Pierce. Surely you don't believe everything ends well." She knew his story and it hadn't ended well. Now, of course, he and Raul were with a company they liked and did work they liked, but their Navy careers had ended badly.

"No, I don't believe everything ends well, but for the moment, our mission is to prove that the video is a deepfake and that everyone needs to step back. That's a mission we can't allow to fail. But you're going to need to be rested and fed to complete the mission. So eat."

That made sense. They had powerful people arrayed against them. She was counting on Pierce and Jacob Black, but they were also counting on her to be convincing. Even though, at the moment, she wasn't entirely convinced the sky was blue.

A distraction. That's what she needed. Putting a forkful of peppers in her mouth, she smiled at Pierce. "So tell me about yourself."

His eyebrows rose, probably SEAL-speak for surprise. "Are we sure we have exhausted you? Because me? Nothing much to tell."

"You sailed through SEAL training, which is supposedly the toughest in the world. Best of your class, Emma says Raul says. Top marks in ... what would you call it? Gunmanship?"

He was holding back a smile. "Sharpshooting."

"Right. That. My understanding is that no one sails through Hell Week. You end up gasping and limping."

"But standing." He inclined his head.

"And I was told you are an amazing driver, which I saw first-hand. That particularly impresses me because I am a lousy driver. And I don't actually have a car at the moment because there's a bus that drops me off at work and lets me off a block from home." She pointed her fork at him. "Don't ever let me drive."

"God, no!" He recoiled in horror. "No one takes the wheel but me. Did you guys have a seminar on me?"

She smiled. "No. But Hope and Emma are fond of you and speak of you often. Emma says Raul claims you are the finest man he knows. And the trickiest."

Pierce winced. "That's because I spent a year undercover. And lied every second of every day of that year. I hated it."

Riley knew better than to ask where he'd been undercover.

All she knew was that he had done something incredibly dangerous and had come away with enough information to shut down a big terrorist cell.

"Yeah, she said that too. And that you try really hard not to lie, ever."

His face was tight. "I had enough lying to last ten lifetimes."

"Oh man, yeah. I hate lying, too." She nodded. "It gives cognitive dissonance, which can be painful. In my line of work you can't lie. Seeing clearly, seeing reality, and reporting it as accurately as possible is the basis of my job. Anyone who lies would be out on his or her ear. And wouldn't be able to do the job."

"Which is why you find the deepfakes so awful."

"God, yes. Not to mention dangerous. We're in for a world of hurt if we don't deal with the deepfake problem. No one will be able to read reality. Imagine not ever knowing if a photo or a video is real or fake. Never being able to trust your eyes. It would be horrible. And incredibly dangerous. So—what does tomorrow look like?"

If he found the change of subject surprising, he gave no sign of it. "I don't know. I do know we're going to show what you showed us to some people in positions of power. And you're going to explain it to them, like you explained it to us."

Riley cleared her throat delicately. "In my experience, being in a position of power doesn't necessarily mean you're smart or even perceptive."

"No shit. Sorry." Pierce grimaced, but Riley agreed with him. *No shit* was absolutely right. "But still, there have to be people left who'd like to stop a war."

She sighed. "Let's hope so." As long as she could stay alive long enough to convince them.

As if he could read her mind, Pierce learned forward. Took her hand. She discovered she loved it when he did that. Hand-holding got a bum rap. Sappy, only for little kids. Instead, it was great. His hand was so strong and so warm, it seemed to infuse her with strength. There was this instant human connection, the very symbol of *you are not alone in this*. Which for Riley, who'd always been alone, was magical.

Not to mention that when Pierce held her hand, she not only felt the human connection, but she also felt tingles and heat all up her arm.

"Nothing's going to happen to you," he said, face sober and serious. "Guaranteed."

"The other day a small meteorite fell in Italy. Can you protect me from them? One of these days an extinction-event comet will fall to earth and no one will be able to protect anyone."

Surprisingly, Pierce lifted her hand to his mouth. "I'd put you in a bunker. Find some way to keep you safe."

His lips were warm and soft, surprisingly so for such a hard man. Riley forgot to breathe as he kissed the back of her hand. That, too, was old-fashioned. Actually, no one had ever kissed her hand. She'd spent time in France, and the computer nerds she'd been studying with were as far from hand-kissing as it was possible to be. Hand-kissing was no longer in with French men, but apparently it still was with US SEALs.

There was complete silence in the room. Riley realized that all evening the house had been silent. Probably due to special cladding, making it bullet proof or impenetrable to infrared. Or maybe even both. Certainly the windows would be bullet resistant and thus sound-proof. Black Inc. was known to have top notch everything. It felt like they were in a vault somewhere far away from the normal hubbub of Washington, DC. DC was a busy city—crowded, with horrendous traffic, constant sirens as bigwigs crossed the city with police escorts. But right now, it was as if they were outside DC, on some island somewhere far, far away.

A place far from the insanity and violence and greed of the world.

Just the two of them, adrift and remote, in some incredibly peaceful place.

Riley held her breath as she took in Pierce's features. So very handsome, but not aware of his looks at all. Handsome men, in her experience, preened, but not Pierce. He seemed to be fiercely focused on her, staring into her eyes as he kept her hand at his mouth.

Riley had a moment of utter vulnerability, and realized she was about to throw herself into his arms. Because she was attracted, her hormones were clamoring to get close to him, practically demanded it, but also because he seemed so strong and invincible. A haven when her life was at risk.

Those broad shoulders and strong arms were practically designed to shelter and protect and she yearned to be held by him.

But this was crazy. She was his *job*. They weren't on a date, he was sent to protect her. Throwing herself at him would embarrass them both. She winced at the idea of him taking her arms from around his neck, talking her down, trying to be kind.

He was just doing his job, and she was projecting silly girlish ideas onto him. Because she was scared. Well, time to put on her big-girl pants. She was alone, like she'd always been, but she had Pierce and his company and the Black Inc. resources at her disposal. They weren't there to hold her hand, they were here to keep her safe. That's all she should want. To be safe.

Pierce released her hand and then, to her surprise, ran his thumb between her eyebrows. Yeah, she must be frowning like crazy.

"Lots of complicated thoughts circling around this beautiful head."

Riley ruthlessly repressed that little spurt her heart gave when he called her 'beautiful.' It was politeness, that's all.

She rose, forced herself to smile. "Not too many complicated thoughts at all. I've done all that I can do, and just hope someone listens. It's out of my hands. I'm exhausted and I think I am going to go to bed. Let me help you clean up—"

"Absolutely not." Pierce rose, too, and she had to crane her neck to look him in the eyes. "I'll take care of this. You get some rest, you're going to need it in the next few days."

Surprisingly, for someone who was in the prediction line, Riley couldn't think ahead to everything that was coming. She couldn't think back to the past two days and to this horrible morning and she couldn't think ahead to all the powerful men and women she'd have to convince, probably making a bunch of enemies. The only thing she could think about was the present. Right now. So close to Pierce she could feel his body heat, so close she was tempted to reach out and put her arms around him, just to be near to that heat and that strength.

She took a step back. He followed her lead and took a step back, too.

"I'll walk you to your room," he said. It made her smile. He said it as if there were lions and tigers and bears on the way to her room. But she didn't say no. Any moment spent with him was pleasurable, his presence alone reassuring that the world still made a little bit of sense, even after the day she'd had.

At the door to her bedroom, she stopped, turned around. Lifted her head, surprised all over again at how tall he was. "I'll—ah—I'll see you tomorrow morning."

He dipped his head solemnly.

"Sleep well." Two short words, delivered in his deep voice, reverberated in her belly. Man, time to retreat.

"Thanks, you too."

Inside the bedroom, she leaned back against the closed door and blew out a breath. She didn't have enough trouble with all the police officers in the world and a security company known for its brutality after her?

She had to have inappropriate hots for a man sent by her friends across the country to help her. The last thing she wanted to do was to embarrass him and embarrass herself.

Finally, her heart stopped pounding and with that, all energy left her body. A search of the chest of drawers produced several lightweight pajamas that looked really comfortable. She chose the top one. It was soft, pure cotton. Light green. She couldn't have chosen better herself. As she'd seen before, the bathroom was full of hotel-size toiletries for men and women and about ten brand-new toothbrushes.

The bed was super comfortable. She pulled out her tablet from the backpack she'd picked up from her apartment. There were something like three thousand books in there, mostly thrillers. Some contemporary history books, and a few romances for when she was feeling particularly lonely.

She opened up the thriller she was reading, but it was less far-fetched than her real life at the moment. A page or two failed to capture her attention. She switched the tablet and the light off and lay back.

She'd slept badly last night, knowing something very bad was brewing. And now that it had boiled over, she was afraid she wouldn't sleep tonight, either, which would make her a wreck tomorrow.

But ... given the dangers in the air, how could she sleep? So much to worry about. Henry's death. The fact that she was somehow being blamed for it. The Sommers Group gunning for her. The *police* gunning for her. Her job was most probably gone.

A war, brewing. On the basis of a lie. War was so frightening.

Riley knew wars had been waged in her lifetime but they had always been far away. War with enemies who didn't have the ability to project power beyond their borders. Wars other people fought. Soldiers who had been trained. The closest she ever came to war was the headlines in the newspapers. In fact, Pierce was the first veteran she'd ever met.

So war was something basically abstract. Something that happened elsewhere, to other people.

But war with China ... there was a whole subreddit on war with China, with thousands of contributions. Speculation. What China could do even before hurling missiles or invading.

It was an open secret among those interested in computer science and computer security that the US was vulnerable to cyberwarfare. There were reams of studies—and even more, thousands of books—dedicated to this.

China could make the US go dark. No more anything. No more electricity, no more internet. No more cars, no more gas. And after a week or two, no more medicine, no more hospitals, no more schools.

How many novels had she read where civilization just stopped. Thousands of years of progress simply wiped out.

And that was just cyberwarfare. There were other fun types of war. Missiles, invasions. And the Big One.

Nuclear.

What to worry about first? Problems buzzed in her head and were going to buzz there all night and she'd get up with that bombed-out feeling, eyes full of sand, reflexes shot to hell, brain all gummed up. Totally incapable of functioning. Acting like a zombie.

She twisted and turned restlessly, throwing the covers back then pulling them up again.

Oh God, this was going to be a sleepless night.

She turned her head on the pillow, riddled with anxiety, and went out like a light.

"RILEY." The voice is deep, deep, like it comes from the bowels of hell. Containing eons of pain and horror.

She looks around but there is no one. Vast emptiness, all around. No one in sight. Only shifting gray shadows.

"Riley." That voice again. Deep, echoing. Fading.

She looks down and the bottom drops out of her world. Henry. Lying in a pool of blood. Sprawled on his back, face etched with pain.

She drops to her knees, frantically touching him all over. She can't see a wound but the pool of blood keeps spreading. Her hands are red, her knees soaked in his blood.

"Riley ..." he says on a rattling breath.

"Oh God, I'll get help, Henry! You need help! You're bleeding!"

Her hands can't find where the blood is coming from. With difficulty, Henry lifts one of his hands, covered in blood, and stills her hands.

"Too late ... Riley. Too ... late for me. Stop them. Stop ... them." The words come between pained breaths. His voice holds all the sadness in the world. The voice of a man who has nothing left.

She is frantic. "Stop who, Henry? Who?" She brushes his straight black hair back so she can see his eyes. Even his hair is soaked in blood.

But it is too late. Henry's dark eyes cloud over, his head falls back, comes to rest on the ground, in the blood, and he doesn't move.

He is gone.

"Henry!" she screams, but he isn't answering. Will never answer again.

His right hand is lying on the ground, smeared with blood, palm up. His index finger is pointed away from him, toward a dark roiling cloud. Toward a darkness. He wants her to go somewhere. There. Of course she will. She will go anywhere he indicates. She will do this one last thing for him.

Rising, Riley moves in the direction of the finger, toward the dark cloud. Tiny flashes, like lightning, glimmer in the cloud. The cloud roils, restless. Foreboding grips her guts. With each step, it is as if she is walking closer and closer to her doom. Her steps falter, feet heavy. It is as if this were a planet with heavier gravity, every step an effort. She can barely pick her feet up. She shuffles. It is so hard to walk.

It is so hard to breathe. The air gets heavier, hotter. And yet, it is snowing. Snowing? She holds out her hand. Something small and gray and greasy falls into her palm. Then two, then three. They crumble when she touches them. Filthy snowflakes? No. Ashes, floating in the gray, sodden sky.

At first a few flakes, then more and more, a cloud of them. The ground is muddy and uneven underfoot. Her feet stick to the ground. It is hard to keep her balance, and she is terrified of falling. There are cracks in the ground, long and deep. She's terrified of falling into one of the cracks. They yawn open, dark and bottomless.

She is alone. There is no one else. It feels like there is no one else alive in the world besides her. They are all dead. How can anyone even breathe with all this ash in the air? She coughs.

A wind lifts, hot and noxious. The ash swirls, at times masking the landscape, at times unveiling it. When the ash clears for a moment, she sees that there is nothing there—a flat, dun- colored, featureless plain that stretches on forever.

But—there! In the distance. A puff of dust that grows, climbs higher, becomes a monstrous mushroom cloud. A horrific boom that shakes the earth. Blinding light. The wind lifts, growing.

The wind will grow and will sweep her away. She is about to die.

The ashes form a face in the translucent sky. Gaunt, cruel. Huge dead eyes, a mouth that opens. "Riley," it whispers in a deep bass voice. "Everyone will die and it's all your fault." The dead eyes sweep the landscape and the wind picks up, blowing so hard she has to dig her feet into the soft, damp earth. There is nothing to cling to. The wind will soon annihilate her.

She is crying because it's true. Humanity is gone. And it's all her fault.

"Riley!" Another voice booms and a hand reaches out from nowhere to touch her.

She screams, but no sound comes out of her throat. She thrashes, desperately trying to get away from the hand that wants to drag her down, down.

"Riley, wake up!"

She screams again, in vain.

Riley pulls her arms over her face, to protect herself against the monster, scrabbling with her legs to get away. She makes horrific sounds, desperate to get away, to escape her imminent death.

Strong arms surround her, a type of strength she cannot fight. She is strong but not strong like this.

It is the end.

"Honey, stop!" The arms tighten around her. But they aren't hurting her. Just holding her in an unbreakable grip. "Don't fight me, Riley. You're having a nightmare."

The words don't make any sense, nothing makes sense except this exceptional strength holding her.

She can't fight her way free; she needs one moment of freedom before dying. A scream dies in her throat, throttling her.

Help! She screams but it comes out a whisper. Help!

"I'm here," the voice answers. "Riley, I'm here. Open your eyes."

She opens her eyes and sees ... safety. Shelter. Protection.

Pierce.

8

P ierce was used to sleeping lightly on missions. Even in sleep, he was always ready for action. But it wasn't necessary now, because there were Black Inc. men standing guard and there were none better. They would be alert, on guard all night. He knew that. Knew he could relax. He needed to get his sleep, and the men were there so he and Riley could rest, knowing they were safe.

But there was something about this situation that just riled him. Made him angry. He wasn't in any way unaware of the situation. It was fucked. Things had already deteriorated so much that he felt like the country was racing toward war. He knew exactly the kind of people in power who were not unhappy about the pretext for war. Who wouldn't care that the video was a deepfake. They thought they could keep it on this side of a hot war. Test out some new missiles, new drone technology, test their cybersecurity. Write their names in the textbooks that would be used at military academies in the future. Make their names. Make some money. It was all good.

They were crushingly wrong, of course, and the world could be left a nuclear wasteland if it got out of hand.

War getting out of hand was practically a given. Almost in the playbook.

And those same fuckers were exactly the ones after Riley, whose only guilt was to be too smart, too good at her job. So they stretched those greedy mouths of theirs wide to gobble her right up with sharply pointed teeth. Chew her up and spit out the bones like some monstrous dragon of old.

Not going to happen.

They would get Riley quite literally over his dead body. But big power situations ate people like him and Riley right up. He would sacrifice his life to keep her safe, but it was no guarantee at all that she could stop this momentum. And that they wouldn't somehow engineer a trial for murder, if they didn't kill her.

It was a shitshow all around, and visions of a dead Riley, a wounded Riley and—since he made a point of being honest with himself—Riley running like a gazelle, Riley climbing up the wall of a building like a beautiful Spiderman, kept him awake.

Every once in a while he did a sensory scan of the environment. Listening for any sounds that shouldn't be there, checking the security cameras on his cell.

He knew there was a security system in place, but still.

In one of the scans, he heard something and sat up. What the ...

Muffled sounds. Not whispers, but groans, like someone in pain. He rose up out of bed, Glock in hand, and opened the bedroom door silently, standing, gun up, beside the wall. The sounds were louder now, muffled moans. Coming from Riley's room.

He stood outside her door, knuckle out, ready to rap, when he heard a painful moan, thought *fuck this*, and opened her door.

She was having a nightmare.

There was light coming in from the street, and he could see her on the bed, tangled in sheets and light summer comforter, tossing her head back and forth, a whine of pain coming from her compressed lips. She was trying to suppress her terror of the nightmare, as her legs scrabbled under the covers, trying to run away from whatever it was that was terrifying her.

Well, professional soldiers and lawmen all gunning for her —that would do it.

He looked down at her for a moment. A full moon and a street lamp cast white light through the window onto her and turned her skin alabaster. She looked like a marble statue, if it weren't for her eyes fluttering behind her lids.

So beautiful. So brave. So terrified.

She moaned behind clenched teeth.

He couldn't stand it a second longer. Putting his Glock on the nightstand, grip towards him, because you never knew, he put a hand on her shoulder. Felt the lean muscle and delicate bone structure under it. A brave, strong woman who could be crushed like a bug by the forces after her.

Not while he drew a breath.

Under his hand, she was trembling lightly. He cupped her shoulder gently, shook her. "Riley," he said. "Wake up."

She gasped, eyes flicking back and forth behind the lids.

"Riley."

Suddenly she thrashed her limbs and emitted a stifled scream, breathing heavily, eyes wide open and terrified

"It's okay." Pierce kept his voice low and calm. "It's okay. It's just me, Pierce. You're having a nightmare. Shhh ..."

Riley lifted herself up on her elbows, eyes so pale they were almost white in the light of the street lamp. "What—"

She was still shaking.

Fuck this.

Pierce slid onto the bed, on top of the covers, and took her in his arms. He turned until she was on top of him and he held a hand to the back of her head and an arm around her waist. The classic protection hold, protecting the vulnerable parts of the body—the head and the viscera. When she calmed, she would feel his heartbeat, which is the single most reassuring thing a human can do. Share a heartbeat.

It didn't help, however, that he went fully erect at the feel of her in his arms. But he would rather tear his own throat out than make a move on her in this vulnerable moment.

"You were having a nightmare," he said, keeping his voice low and calm. "Nightmares are terrifying, particularly when linked to the events of the day or recent events, because there's a tinge of reality. You had a stressful day. I'd be surprised if you didn't have a nightmare. But you're safe. Nothing will happen to you. You can let go."

Because he could feel her stiffness and vigilance. All of a sudden, she relaxed, her body molding with his. Her hip brushed his groin and felt his erection. She stiffened again.

"Don't worry about that." He smiled in the darkness. "It's like an automatic response to holding a beautiful woman in my arms. I have no intention of doing anything about it. All I want is for you to get a good night's sleep."

Riley let out her breath in a whoosh. They lay there, in silence.

When he placed his hand on her narrow back, he could feel her heart rate slowing. Good.

"Do you want to tell me about the nightmare?" he asked quietly. "Sometimes it helps to talk it out." He personally never talked about his own nightmares, but he imagined women would talk it out. Women were more verbal. Used words instead of sex and alcohol to work their way through things. Once, after a particularly vicious firefight, the barracks was full of men moaning and thrashing in their sleep and a heavy silence the next morning.

If they hadn't been in a dry country, a lot of them would have gotten drunk that evening, including him.

She sighed. "It's becoming vague, but I remember the feeling. The feeling of fear and doom. Something bad coming and then something bad right there."

God, that sounded like every nightmare ever.

"Do you remember anything else?" She'd shuddered and he ran his hand down her back. For comfort, and because it was a delight to touch her.

"Henry." Her voice choked.

"What?"

"Henry Yu. My friend and boss. He was on the ground, bleeding, but I couldn't find the wound. The ground beneath him was soaked in blood, but I couldn't staunch his wounds because I couldn't find them. He barely had breath to talk. He said to stop them, but I didn't know who. Just that I had to stop them. The air was hot, hard to breath. Then Henry died and I walked and walked, through mud and ash. Then there was a mushroom cloud on the horizon, and a hot wind and ... and then you woke me up."

There was silence. "Well," Pierce said finally. "Not hard to interpret."

"No. I'm terrified it might come true."

He couldn't say anything. This was one smart lady. Reassuring her that the worst wouldn't happen would be insulting to her intelligence. The fact was that he was terrified, too, that the nightmare might come true.

One thing being a SEAL had taught him was that wishing something wouldn't happen wasn't any kind of a plan. Shit happened. Shit happened really often.

"Do you—do you have nightmares?" Her voice was the merest whisper in the night.

Oh fuck. What to say? Pierce didn't like spending the whole night with women because of this. But she deserved the truth. "All the time, actually. I have nightmares all the time. Several times a week I dream of my commanding officer shooting a pregnant woman in the stomach and watching her die, screaming, in a dusty street. While he smiled. It took her a long time to die, and I see that in my dreams. Nightmares."

"Emma told me the story," she whispered into his chest.

He nodded. "Yeah."

"I'm so sorry."

Her head lifted and fell with his big sigh.

"You've earned your own nightmare. But we're going to put it right. You've got ASI and Black Inc. and your brainiac friends on your side."

"And you," she said softly.

His arms tightened. "And most definitely me."

Pierce knew his limitations. He wasn't a geopolitical genius, he didn't own a company that ran with the big boys. Nothing he could ever say could change government policy. He was a soldier, an operator and a good one, but he didn't have any political power. So he wasn't the one who was going to have to go to the top guys and convince them to call off the dogs. But by God he was going to keep her safe while his company and Jacob Black did their thing. It was not going to be a case where in the end right prevailed, but whoops! The wrong person got whacked. Nope, she was going to stay safe.

"Pierce?" Her voice was a little slurred. She was falling back asleep.

"Hmm?"

"I'm really glad I have you."

God. His arms tightened again and he had to work to loosen

them. Because he wanted to hold her close, hug her so tightly she could fit inside him and he could keep her as safe as safe could be.

"Yeah." His voice was rough and he coughed to loosen it up.

He was going to say something else, but she'd fallen asleep.

RILEY WAS USED to waking up fast, refreshed and ready for the day. Instead, she came up slowly, in swoops.

Each step was wonderful, and she'd linger there for long moments.

First off, she was lying on something hard and warm. Most hard things were cold, but not this. Nope. It was like lying on a heater, only contoured. Shaped in a way that she could fit perfectly. She moved her head and discovered that it was lying on that hard surface but with, like, a grassy mat.

Hmmm.

Her internal clock said it was about five a.m. The sky was pewter, lightening by the minute. There should be some urban noises, traffic, music somewhere, but the place was really sound-proofed.

There was utter silence in the room, completely different from her own apartment, which had traffic noise, barking dogs and usually kids' voices. Now it was a magical silence except for a dull, regular thudding. Reassuring. The most reassuring sound on Earth. A heartbeat, right under her ear.

And oh, yum. This amazing smell. Soap and shampoo and oddly enough, a touch of leather. Totally enticing, coming from all that heat and hardness.

She was lying on a human being. A male. Pierce. And it was the most pleasurable surface imaginable.

He was holding her tightly, both arms around her back and she was half on, half off him and she never wanted to move.

Wanted to stay in this position forever. Warm and comfortable and protected.

There was Pierce and her and nothing else in the world. Just the two of them

She hadn't made a sound and hadn't moved, but all of a sudden, his arms tightened.

"You awake?" His voice was low, deep. She could feel the vibrations of his voice in his chest, the first time she'd ever felt that.

"Yes," she sighed. "How could you tell?"

She could *hear* his smile though she couldn't see his face. Which was a pity because it was a really nice face. But she could see two amazing pecs covered in chest hair, which was just as nice.

"The air around you changed."

"Oh yeah?" What a charming thought. That the air around you changed, depending on whether you were awake or asleep.

"Mmm-huh. How are you feeling?"

"Surprisingly good, considering."

"Considering?"

"Well, we could be going to war and I might be wanted for murder."

His hand lifted and covered the back of her head, running his fingers through her hair. Massaging her scalp. Oh, man. She felt like purring.

"I think you can stop worrying about being arrested. Jacob talked to local law enforcement and I think they realized you couldn't have shot Henry Yu. When this is over, I expect you might have to go into the local police department and testify, but there won't be any consequences."

"Thank you."

"Thank Jacob. But I don't think he's expecting thanks. He

was angry as hell that that was even on the table and spoke quietly with a couple of high-up police brass."

She lay on him for a minute or two. Let that fear float away. But the other one remained.

It was so horrific. She'd worked in national security all her working life, and part of what she'd done at NSA was construct scenarios. If this, then that. War scenarios were common. They were usually for minor skirmishes or conflicts that might interrupt maritime shipping for a while or empty out a part of some third world city or interfere with trade for a month or two. Serious, but not lethal.

But sometimes those scenarios became more serious. Touched upon consequences to the Homeland. Scenarios where whole sections of the country experienced famine and chaos. Where medical care completely broke down. Food supplies were totally interrupted. Scenarios where hundreds of thousands died.

Those were the serious scenarios but not the most serious. Those were nuclear. She'd been part of a massive study of the potential effects of nuclear warfare and it had been devastating. The estimates were of a 90% reduction in food production and the death within a year of five billion people. Making the Black Death look like a summer picnic.

And then, later—the total breakdown of civilization. The people who lived would envy the dead. No more travel, no more medical care, no more education. No more cities. No food or medicine. No books or theater or films. The next five or six generations would grow up completely illiterate, completely without art or science. It was entirely possible they would live in caves. Everyone would suffer from radiation sickness and die young.

Riley's heart broke when she read the scenario because she could imagine it all, very clearly.

"Hey," Pierce said gently. "Don't think about it. I'm not going to say that everything's gonna be all right. You're a smart woman and you know that is not always true. But what is true is that you can't change most of what is happening or going to happen. There are a lot of factors in play besides the truth. Your job will be to convince people that you are right, and the more rested you are, the better you'll be able to do that."

She shook her head. "So basically, lying here in bed is doing my country a great service?"

Riley twisted her head to look up at him. His face was serious, with a slight uptilt to his mouth. He believed what he said, but even he recognized it was ridiculous. But true.

She sighed and rested her head back against that glorious chest.

He placed his hand under her loose pajama top and ran his fingers softly up and down her back. It felt wonderful, as if his hands had magic properties. Maybe they did. Maybe that was a particular SEAL attribute—Magic Hands.

"You're still tense." It was so amazing to hear his words but also *feel* them vibrating in his chest. She was tempted to ask him to recite something long, like *Casey at the Bat* or the lyrics to *American Pie*. And just lie back and feel those deep vibrations against her cheek, without listening to the words. His hand going up and down and up and down and up and ... down. That huge hand slipped under the PJ bottoms and caressed her buttocks.

It was very forward of Pierce. Mmmm. She should say something. And she would ... soon. But oh God, that felt good. She found herself moving her ass in time with his hand, and the more flesh his hand covered, the better it felt.

And she dropped all pretense with herself. She wanted this. She wanted it badly. Her right hand was over his left pec and he covered her hand with his. Then he laced his hand through her fingers. The other hand continued its exploratory path over her back.

It might be considered raw stress relief. She'd been chased, shot at, hounded. She'd had to put together a technical presentation that could be understood by tech Neanderthals. So a little sex could be considered perfect to release all that tension. Sex notoriously engendered endorphins—feel good hormones.

But it wasn't that. She didn't want just a penis with a person attached. She wanted him, Pierce. And only him. This man who'd saved her and who had slotted into her life so quickly and so well.

The man who had unquestioningly shouldered all her burdens, while doing his best to protect her.

A man who got her, maybe because he was friends with her friends. Her friends had found their soul mates. Men who *got* them. All of them—Felicity, Hope, Emma and Riley herself—were brainy but sadly lacking in feminine wiles. They'd never learned the art of manipulation. What you saw was what you got. For many men, they were too much to handle. But not for Metal, Luke, Raul and now Pierce.

Pierce hadn't once acted as if he thought she was a freak. And as for her—she was completely taken. He was handsome, yes. Built, for sure. Competent in many things. Straightforward, easy to be with. But more than that, there was this magical component to him. As if he'd come from another, much better planet. Where they grew fabulous men. She felt safe and excited, both, at once.

So yes, she wanted this.

The hand caressing her backside went lower. She shifted her legs, opened to him. An invitation.

He took it, cupping her. The hand slipped between her buttocks and covered her core. One finger penetrated her core and her breath stopped from excitement.

She lifted her head, expecting to maybe find him looking smug, smoldering. But instead he looked incredibly serious, face drawn, nostrils white with some kind of tension.

He swallowed heavily. "Is this okay?"

The heat in her throat was so great she found it hard to get the words out. Finally, she just nodded.

"I need the words," he said, still not smiling, still looking like he was in pain.

"Yes," she finally got out. "God yes."

He finally smiled, but it wasn't a relieved grin. It was more like a ... a communication. He stared straight into her eyes and the smile was like a pact between him and her. *This is what we both want.*

She lifted herself up, her face close to his. He kept his eyes on her, looking so intently it was as if he were looking inside her soul. It was too intense and she closed her eyes as he kissed her.

Their first kiss.

It was brief, so intense it almost hurt, like an electrical charge. His mouth lifted almost immediately and he looked at her, unsmiling.

In the absolute quiet of the room, something was happening. Through the windows, the sun had come up, a streak of light illuminating the room. A new day, a new beginning.

He lifted his head again and this time the kiss was long and deep and unbearably arousing. His finger penetrated her just as his tongue touched hers and it was as if she'd been touched by a prod.

She sucked in a breath but he was kissing her, so she sucked in air from his lungs. Breathing through him.

Another kiss, even deeper, finger caressing her sex.

There were small noises and she realized that she was wet, almost embarrassingly so. Super turned on. More turned on than she was during actual sex with other men. The finger imitated a penis, thrusting in and out and she was so turned on it felt like she was burning up, from the inside. She moaned against his mouth and he reached deep inside her, touched something and oh! She just blew up in a flash of heat and light, clenching around him over and over until the orgasm blew through her and subsided.

She'd lost contact with the world for a moment, so she didn't notice that she'd been lifted and turned around. Pierce settled on her, opening her legs with his own. His weight and strength on her felt so delicious.

It was hard, but she managed to open her eyes and saw his face, right above hers. He was watching her so intently, as if to catch the most minute expression of hesitation or rejection.

God no. Nothing had ever felt so good and she wanted more.

Pierce lifted himself up on one arm and unbuttoned her pajama top, watching his fingers working the buttons as if doing something incredibly hard and tricky, like defusing a bomb.

If that orgasm just by being touched was any indication, another bomb was going off soon. He spread the panels until she was naked and just looked at her.

"You are so beautiful," he said. "Just perfect."

Her hands were cupped on his shoulders, strong and broad. *You're not so bad yourself,* she thought, but couldn't say. Her throat had seized up, as a wave of heat washed over her, head to foot.

Pierce bent his dark head and licked a nipple. She shook, exhaled slowly as he suckled. There was an electric line directly linking her breast and her sex and as he tugged at her breast, there was an echo in her vagina. She clenched around the finger still in her, hard.

Pierce breathed in sharply. His face was stark, drawn, flushed over the cheekbones. All his muscles were taut.

"I can't wait any more, Riley. Just can't."

She couldn't talk, but she nodded. He leaned over, opened

the nightstand drawer, grabbed a condom and smoothed it over himself.

He rolled onto her again and she welcomed him with every cell of her body, arms and legs open. And when he slid into her, he could tell that she welcomed him there, too. She was slick, and he entered deep at the first thrust.

They stilled, both of them. Pierce on top, faces an inch apart. They studied each other. They were as close as two human beings could be. Riley had never had sex as intimate as this, as if they were one being in two bodies.

She was still reeling from her earlier orgasm and didn't want to move. It would be sensory overload. Already every inch of skin felt imprinted by him, incredibly pleasured by him.

Pierce raised himself on his forearms and started moving in her. Slowly at first, then faster and faster, until the bed was rocking and the headboard beat against the wall.

She loved it, loved every second of it, loved the feel of him inside her, loved the strength she felt over every inch of his body. Loved the feeling of the two of them wrapped up in each other, the whole world shut out.

He was moving so fast in her now, so deeply. She couldn't figure out where she finished and he began. Pierce reached down, pulled her legs up and far apart so he could reach even more deeply inside her and she locked her ankles in the small of his back, riding his hips as he rode her.

It was so intense it couldn't last. She gave a small cry, arched her back and started contracting around him, but she was coming with every cell of her body. The breath in her lungs, her thighs, her breasts …

Pierce gave a great shout and started coming too, in a frenzy of movement so strong it was a miracle she didn't burst into flames. She clung to him, her raft in a sea of sensation.

Oh God, so this was sex? Why hadn't anyone told her?

Nothing could have prepared her for these roiling emotions, for this feeling of having given her body to Pierce. For his body being hers.

He slumped on her with his full weight, head against her shoulder, as both of them gasped and shuddered, aftershocks of the orgasms shaking them both.

Oh man, Pierce's weight anchored her just as sleep tugged her down too. She was going down, down, down...

An annoying buzzing sound. What was that? This place was soundproofed.

It was on and on, interrupting her incredibly pleasurable free fall.

Buzz, buzz, buzz.

"Argh." She was too wiped out to be able to produce words, but she could make a sound of intense displeasure. "Mmph."

Above her, Pierce gave a great sigh and lifted himself up and away.

She missed him immediately, his heat and power. Without opening her eyes, she frowned and held her arms out.

"Sweetheart, we have to get up." That was Pierce's deep voice, but the words weren't making any sense.

Get up? No way.

She pulled her hand out from under the blanket and wagged her index finger from side to side.

No.

Was he crazy?

"Darling." Pierce kissed her shoulder. "I hate to do this, but we have to go."

Her eyes popped open. "Go? Go where?"

He'd stopped smiling.

"We have to go save the world."

9

The cardinal rule of close protection was—don't get personally involved with the person you are protecting. It was a rule for a reason. Pierce was continually distracted, his gaze turning constantly to Riley sitting beside him. It was all him, too. She definitely wasn't trolling for his attention. In fact, she was going over her presentation to make sure it was perfect.

He found it so hard to keep his eyes off her. As a man, he was fascinated. As an operator, he was appalled at his behavior. She was here, in an armored vehicle and he was at the wheel. Inside the car there was no danger to her. Zero. Zilch. All the danger would come from outside the vehicle, which is where his attention should be. Instead of stealing glances at her every ten seconds.

He had to unfuck his head, STAT.

He shouldn't be even thinking that word, because it reminded him of this morning, in bed. Of sliding into her hot tightness. He moved uneasily in his seat. Jesus, he hadn't had sex in what? Six months? They'd been really busy and he hadn't missed it and his dick had just stayed down. And now, it wanted up, it wanted to be in Riley Robinson. And it wanted more of that, lots more. It wanted Riley.

Who was staring into the monitor of her magic laptop.

"Who are we seeing this morning?" Riley asked the question without looking at him, attention totally focused on her laptop.

Pierce wanted to sigh, but didn't. She was absolutely right to stay on the business of the morning.

"We're going to meet with General MacBride and Colonel Perry and their adjuncts. And then we might be kicked upstairs. They are drawing up an OPLAN, an—"

"Operations Plan, yes I know," she replied. And he was reminded she'd worked in security for a year at the NSA.

"I think it is going to take a concerted effort across the board, both in the Pentagon and in Congress."

She looked up at that. "So we're going to do this dog-and-pony show a couple of times?"

"Over and over. Sorry."

She sighed. "No. If that's what it takes. And we're fighting against an accepted narrative, which is also hard. But it's a narrative that can lead to war and is definitely worth combating."

Pierce took her hand and brought it to his mouth. "And we're going to do this while keeping you safe."

She gave a faint smile. "Easier said than done."

"Nope."

Pierce turned his head and looked her right into the eyes, those remarkable pale eyes, so intelligent and sad. He was not going to lose her.

Though they were in danger, he felt that something was starting, something big. He could try to keep his head out of his pants, but he couldn't keep it out of his heart.

This morning hadn't been just some sex to let off steam. He'd felt a connection he'd never felt before, some kind of flow, some kind of woo-woo thing he'd never believed in, even though his buddy Raul said the instant he saw Emma he 'knew'. *Knew what*, he'd asked his buddy. *That she was the one*, Raul had said and secretly Pierce thought he was batshit crazy. But now ...

"Nothing's going to happen to you. Lotta guys working really hard to keep you safe."

Riley looked stricken. "I know. I'm really sorry."

With reluctance, Pierce gave her hand back to her. "God no. Don't apologize! None of this is your fault. You're trying to right a wrong, and in this world, that's always hard."

The lead car started veering off to the right, before the Pentagon turnoff at 8C, and Pierce followed. There was no public parking at the Pentagon, though he supposed Black could have gotten them a special permit.

"This isn't the way to the main entrance," Riley said.

"Nope. We're going in through a side entrance." He glanced at her. "Less fuss."

"You don't think the Sommers Group might have drones using facial recognition?"

"I expect he has blanketed the city with drones and has hacked into security cameras, but not over the Pentagon. I don't think he'd dare. And this is an area that official Washington more or less agrees is off-limits to law enforcement. So you're okay."

"How tech savvy do you think the people we're going to talk to are? It's important, otherwise it'll just feel like I'm feeding them a line in gobbledygook."

Pierce sighed. "I don't know. I think Jacob chose the audience because of their pull, not their tech savvy. But there will be adjuncts in the room who should be able to follow you." Though secretly, he doubted many people in the military were as proficient as Riley. Or Felicity, Hope and Emma, for that matter. But they had to convince those with war-making powers, whether they could follow the tech or not.

Pierce was following the lead car to a small car park. He pulled up beside the lead car and killed the engine. The trailing car pulled in beside him. He put his weapon in the console between the seats, checked with the other drivers and they all got out at the same time.

He circled his vehicle and opened the door for Riley. He needed to keep his hands free, so he didn't help her down, but she definitely didn't need help, jumping down nimbly, backpack already in place. Each vehicle had two operators, the driver and the one riding shotgun. They immediately surrounded Riley in a diamond formation and moved off. Riley didn't need instructions to stay right in the middle, she did it instinctively.

They moved in formation to a small building adjacent to the River Terrace Entrance, entering a lobby. The guy at the desk wasn't some supermall time-server retired cop. He was young, fit, alert, behind a bulletproof screen.

Pierce was prepared. He held out his ASI ID and nodded to the other four, who pulled out their Black Inc. IDs. Riley showed her NSA badge. The security guy studied each one carefully, not smiling, checked it against a list he had, then nodded toward the elevator behind him, and buzzed them through the gate. First they walked through a metal detector then went to the elevator.

The elevator took them four stories underground. Guidebooks all said that the Pentagon only had two underground stories, but that was bullshit. Riley again was in the center of a phalanx of operators, quietly waiting to reach their destination.

Down a corridor, to the right, and there was another unsmiling security guard who scrutinized their IDs, checked his list, and opened a heavy steel door for them. They walked in in twos, Pierce and Riley in the middle.

It was a war room, though not big. An oval, shiny, mahogany conference table, a wall-sized flat screen, laptops at each seat. General MacBride sat at the head of the table, Colonel Perry to his left side. Pierce didn't recognize the other officers, though by their uniforms they were another two colonels and a captain. Several young men and women sat in chairs against the walls. They didn't look hard and tough like the military officers. They looked dewy and soft. But they also looked like they would understand Riley more than the officers.

Jacob Black sat at the right hand of General MacBride.

There were name plates and Riley's was in the middle of the table, facing the huge wall screen. She sat, set up her laptop. Pierce and his teammates stood in the back of the room against a wall. They weren't needed for this. Everyone waited until Riley was done, and then General MacBride cleared his throat and bent toward the microphone in front of him. It was a directional mike and he didn't need to bend toward it, but old habits die hard.

"Good morning," the General said. "I have called you all in to listen to Dr. Riley Robinson, who has, I am told, pertinent information on the ongoing crisis with the People's Republic of China. I have done so upon the insistence of Jacob Black, who has been ... persuasive." He shot a sour glance at Black, who didn't change expression. "So, Dr. Robinson, I understand you have a presentation for us. These are busy days for us all, as you can imagine, so I'll turn the floor over to you right away."

He capped off his little speech by shooting his cuffs and ostentatiously checking his watch, when the time was shown not only on the huge wall monitor but also on an enormous clock on another wall.

He was trying to intimidate Riley. Luckily, Riley didn't even notice. She looked around the table at each participant. Pierce knew she was nervous, he'd felt her trembling as he put a hand to her back to usher her into the room. He didn't think she was scared of making the presentation, but rather scared that the presentation wouldn't work.

They were in the Pentagon, a huge institution that had started a slow but inexorable push toward war. War was the business of the Pentagon, and there were a lot of people happy at the idea of a war with China. They were sure that they could contain it, and anyway the people planning it sure weren't the ones who would fight it. A lot of careers were going to be made, and here was Riley, a lone woman, saying *no. Don't do it.*

It was sort of working against her that she was so good-looking. That wasn't the way Pierce thought—the women at ASI were drop-dead gorgeous, every single one, while being serious professionals at the top of their game. He and his teammates respected them. But a lot of men instinctively didn't take a beautiful woman seriously. As if their looks counted against them. And Riley was amazingly beautiful. Serious in demeanor but also seriously beautiful.

However, Pierce was the only one there to know how incredibly gorgeous she was all over. How silky soft her skin was, over strong, slim muscles. How perfect her breasts were, how her breathing speeded up when he kissed those breasts, how she arched when he touched her between her legs, how wet she got...

His groin just lit up.

Fuck.

He shifted uneasily, cursing himself. Goddamn. In a room at the Pentagon with war on the horizon was no place to get a woodie.

"Good morning, everyone." Riley's cool voice made him stand up straight. She had an effect on not just him, but on everyone. The room came to attention. "My name is Riley

Robinson, and just to give you an idea of my credentials, I have a Masters in Computer Science and a double PhD in Statistics and Data Science and Computer Science. I worked for the NSA and I currently work for the NSO. My specific remit at the NSO is analysis of People's Liberation Army footage. I have reviewed perhaps three thousand hours of satellite footage of the People's Liberation Army on maneuvers. Three days ago, some footage from the Democratic Republic of Congo came to my attention. Though to the naked eye it seemed like a video of an attack by PLA soldiers on a group of American scientists, it was clearly corrupted as you can see here, and here and here."

She pressed a button and the wall monitor came to life. It was what he'd seen back at the safe house, only blown up to wall size and 8K. Riley used her laser pointer to show the anomalies she'd shown them back at the safe house. It was all much clearer than it had been before.

Riley waited a second for everyone to absorb the images. "To a trained eye, this video is a deepfake, but it's good enough to create a stir. Deepfakes are an iterative process. You work at it back and forth and it improves. And a few hours later, this is what that video looked like."

On the monitor, the video was crystal clear, sharp in its details. Chinese soldiers attacking Americans. The faces were clear, their uniforms crisp, insignia sharp and visible.

"But," Riley continued, "in real life, this is what that video is, when stripped of the manipulation."

The wall monitor, paused at a dramatic moment in the massacre, rippled as layers were stripped, new layers added on and then the image came into very sharp focus. Only it was completely different.

There was an audible gasp in the room. Pierce watched the brass, looking for anomalies. But the brass all looked shocked.

They understood immediately the import of what they were seeing.

"What was supposedly troops of the PLA attacking American scientists turned out to be operators of the Sommers Group attacking American scientists. In a very rabid fashion. And seemingly unprovoked."

Riley let the video run its course, pausing it at the last minute, before the satellite overhead passed over the horizon.

"As everyone knows, the scientists were part of a research group from the CDC and Yale University, studying emerging viruses. They were gathering samples of what was suspected of being a new strain of Ebola. This video made its way to me because I am considered an expert on Chinese troop movements. But when I realized that the video was a deepfake, I called my boss, Henry Yu, to come look at it. No matter which way you looked at it, it was a political hot potato. Dr. Yu took a copy I made of both videos, and was going to take it upstairs to his boss, Dr. Morris Sartan, but I don't know if he did. Soon after, word came that Dr. Yu was dead of a gunshot wound to the head. I then saw operators from the Sommers Group, heavily armed—and I have no idea how that happened because we walk through metal detectors to get into the NSO—come marching toward my office."

She paused, switched off her mike, drank half a glass of water. Pierce marveled at her cool, realized how scared she must be. But she'd also managed to give the brass some clues. She couldn't follow through, but they sure as hell could. They could find out where Yu had gone, and whether he'd made it to his boss's office.

"I ... ran away from the NSO, and I understand that the Sommers Group is after me. It's ... frightening." By not a flicker of an eyelash did she let on that she was protected by Jacob

Black and four of his men, and by Pierce. She was protecting them.

"Ms. Robinson," General MacBride began.

"Dr. Robinson," Riley answered, and the General's mouth tightened. He wasn't tall, but very broad, with a square blunt face. He was unsmiling, eyes narrowed.

"Forgive me. Of course. Dr. Robinson. That is quite a story you're telling there. But the fact of the matter is, we're in the middle of a geopolitical crisis, and our enemies are escalating. And according to you, it is all because of actions taken by the Sommers Group and not by soldiers of the PLA."

He leaned forward a little, face hard and hostile.

Pierce's cell vibrated slightly and he took it out carefully. He shouldn't be checking his phone during a meeting like this, but there were a lot of balls in the air and he needed to keep on top of everything.

HER ROOM: General MacBride signed a contract to work with the Sommers Group when he retires at the end of the year. The job will pay triple what he earns at the Pentagon.

BLESS the girls in the Her Room back at ASI. Somehow they had found out that General MacBride was in the room and that he was going to be on Adrian Sommers' payroll. Something that he should have said immediately. He had no business staying in this room once Riley accused the Sommers' group operatives of the massacre.

"Dr. Robinson, isn't it possible that the order of things is backward? That Chinese soldiers attacked American scientists and someone tried to turn that video into a deepfake, accusing operators of the Sommers Group? Which, I'll remind the room, is one of our country's biggest and most reputable security companies."

Pierce saw Jacob Black shift in his seat at that.

Riley looked astonished, as if someone had just stated that two plus two makes five. She leaned forward. "General MacBride, the videos are time-stamped. The order is quite clear."

Scowling heavily, the General turned and beckoned to a young aide. The aide sprang forward and they consulted in whispers, the young aide at the end shaking his head adamantly. The General frowned. The aide pointed to the mike and the General tilted his body to the side, but didn't invite the aide to pull up a chair.

"Dr. Robinson, did you run those images through Circle-GAN? For those unfamiliar with the program, it is a generative adversarial network pitting two AIs against each other. It is used not only to generate deepfakes but to spot them."

"No, I did not." Riley gave a small smile. "CircleGAN has a 72% reliability rate. I ran it through a program of my own design, which has a 98% reliability rate."

The aide's face lit up. "Really? What—" Then he noticed the General's deep scowl and he wiped the interest from his face. "Um. So, my understanding is that the data is transmitted in frames. Is that correct?"

Riley nodded. "Yes. That is correct. Each frame is encoded with a Reed-Solomon error-correcting block code. 32 parity bytes are added to every 223 bytes of data. Framing patterns are added, and the resulting stream is encoded with a rate 1/2 constraint-length 7 Viterbi-decoded convolutional error-correcting code. Each bit is converted into a pair of bits that depend on the current bit as well as the previous six bits. The combination of these two codes is called concatenated Reed-Solomon/convolutional coding."

As Riley spoke math, there were five people in the room—two men and three women—who were following, with a great deal of interest. All aides. Everyone else, including the brass, was lost at sea, like him.

But he didn't have to understand convolutional coding, he had to understand the code of human behavior, and while there were those who understood her, and those who admired her without understanding her, there were those who were becoming openly hostile with every passing minute. The General most of all.

"Stop this!" The General pounded the table with his fist. Riley stopped in midstream. Pierce could tell that she had almost forgotten the reason they were here, as she went into the granular details of her job, in nerd heaven. "Dr. Riley, did you know that the People's Republic of China shot a hyper-missile at the *USS Ronald Reagan* two hours ago? Hyper-missiles are capable of penetrating the decks of our aircraft carriers and sinking them. China is escalating and positioning itself for war, while we are here talking about how many pixels can dance on the head of a pin. This is perfectly useless, when we should be drawing up war plans. We are wasting precious time."

He started gathering the briefing papers before him.

But Riley hadn't finished. "I didn't know that the PRC had shot a hyper-missile at the *USS Ronald Reagan*, no sir. I imagine it was in retaliation for our new and massive presence in the Taiwan Strait. The hyper-missile did not penetrate the *Ronald Reagan* because they programmed it that way. The PLA is extremely capable and they would not miss if they wanted to sink the *Ronald Reagan*. We both have the capability of causing massive damage to our militaries and to our countries, not to mention the terrifying prospect of nuclear warfare. It is the terrible consequences of this escalation that leads me to insist that this military escalation is happening as a consequence of a lie. I am a patriot, and if I can possibly stop massive damage to my country, on the basis of a lie, I will do everything in my power to do so."

The General was barely listening and stomped out of the briefing room. But Riley got a lot of sympathetic looks as everyone filed out of the room. Pierce suspected that a lot of them had been convinced by her presentation.

He came away from the wall and put a hand on her shoulder, struck again by the delicacy of her. During the presentation she had seemed a giant, invincible. And yet she wasn't. She was a young woman with no defenses except her excellent mind.

Well ... except for him, his company, and Jacob Black and his company.

"Good job," he said, voice low. "I think you convinced a lot of people."

She looked up at him and he winced at the misery on her face. "Thanks, but I sure didn't convince the General. Though I suspect the two Colonels are rethinking things."

It definitely wasn't the time to tell her about General MacBride's future plans. "I think you convinced more or less everyone but him. Though I don't know how much he understood."

She gave a tired grin and it struck him all at once how taxing these past hours must have been. "Explaining to him stripping the deepfake was like explaining the tax code to a dog."

Pierce coughed to cover the unexpected laugh that blew out of him. In his teens he'd had an amazing merle border collie as smart as they came. Maisie could probably understand more than the General had.

"There's another meeting this afternoon at seventeen hundred hours. That's—"

"Five p.m." She sighed. "Yes. Very familiar with the military clock."

"Sorry."

Riley turned a stricken face to him. "Oh! I didn't mean to be snotty! I'm so sorry. I'm incredibly grateful to you and ASI and Black Inc. You've been ... wonderful." She turned a deep and very pretty shade of pink, and Pierce knew she was thinking about this morning.

He leaned low and whispered in her ear. "You were pretty wonderful yourself."

She turned an even brighter shade of pink. Pierce liked seeing it. She was deathly pale, all this stress taking a terrible toll on her. If a little flirting and the memory of a memorable morning together could put some color in her face, great.

This was the military. Once the meeting was adjourned, the room emptied fast. One of the aides stopped by to introduce himself. Turns out he'd been at MIT several years after she had and they'd had the same professors. Pierce tuned them out once they started talking math. But it was clear that the earnest-looking aide was completely on her side.

Man. It brought back painful memories. He'd loved his time in the Navy. Being a SEAL—having been a SEAL—was embedded bone-deep in his being. He'd loved his teammates, even the scuzzier ones, and he'd grown as close to Raul as to a brother. He loved the discipline, the moving together toward a single goal. The unquestioning help at all times.

But he'd had a lot of boneheaded commanders, besides the psychopath murderer. They'd received orders that didn't always make a lot of sense. That were dangerous, even. As the mission became fuzzier and fuzzier, the orders got crazier and crazier.

The young aide—not a day over twenty-five—was clearly caught between a hard place and a rock. Anyone who could follow what Riley said knew she was telling the truth. And understood that the rush to war was based on a lie. A pernicious, ass-covering one, too.

And then there was the equally appalling idea that some people *wanted that war*. They might not have instigated one, but by God when a perfectly acceptable war presented itself, they weren't going to waste it. And they sure as hell weren't going to let some girl nerd's truth stop them.

The math talk stopped and now it was all *nice to meet you, amazing program you've got there*. The aide departed and Riley checked her cell with a frown. Jacob Black was checking a feed, too.

He stepped to Riley and Pierce. "Riley, that was an exceptional job. I'm going to see if I can advance our meeting at 1700 to 1600 and to see if we can get into the White House this evening. We need to talk to someone who can get to the President."

"It won't be General MacBride," Pierce said sourly, and showed both Black and Riley the message from the HER Room. "They're promising to dig up background info on anyone we speak to."

"Those women are amazing," Black said. "That is very useful intel. I don't need to ask if they are certain?"

"No, you don't need to ask." Riley shook her head. "If they texted it, it's true. And explains a lot." She touched Black's arm. "I have a horrible feeling this is coming to a head, and really bad things will happen before we can have them call off the dogs."

"And before things become too far gone to call them off, even if we convince them it's all a lie."

Riley shut her eyes for a second and sighed.

Pierce looked at Black. "I'm going to take Riley back to the house and feed her and let her rest before the afternoon meetings. I think we'll be testifying all night."

Black nodded. "I'll be in the convoy. We'll escort you and we'll be there when you're ready to leave. In the meantime, I still have some people I'm going to contact."

Getting out of the Pentagon was easier than getting in.

At the convoy, Black slapped the roof of the SUV. "Okay, my guys will be at the safe house at 15.00." He bent a little to address Riley in the shotgun seat. "Riley, be loaded for bear. I think we're getting traction, which means the pushback will be hard."

She nodded and Black stepped away and got into one of the SUVs.

Pierce was ready to roll out when Riley touched him. "Wait."

"Yeah?"

"Do you have a way to communicate with the other two vehicles?"

"Sure. Why?"

"I think we should mix the order up. I think we—you and I —should either be in front or the last in the convoy."

Pierce thought it over. "You know, doctrine has it that the protected vehicle should be protected from the front and the back. Is there a reason not to respect protocol?"

Riley shrugged, looking uneasy. "You think in terms of protocol and military doctrine. I think in terms of mathematical probability. It just seems rational to switch the order on a randomized basis."

Pierce studied her. She was holding up really well in a situation that would have any other civilian screaming and begging to be protected in a bunker. She realized that, for the moment, if the escalation were to stop, it was on her, until they managed to get the big guns on their side.

It was probably just a hunch, but damn it. She had a right to her hunches. His life had been saved twice in the battlespace because he zigged instead of zagged. And even if it wasn't a hunch, if it made her feel better, why not?

He tapped his comms twice, which went out to both vehicles. "Alpha One here, we will be bringing up the rear. Confirm."

"Alpha One, bringing up the rear," came the confirmation.

Alpha Two pulled out, then Alpha Three, then he pulled out too, keeping a regulation distance.

"Thanks, Pierce," she said softly.

"Sure." He knew his voice sounded remote. Usually driving relaxed him, but not when driving in a convoy with the possibility, however remote, of an attack. Then all his senses fired up and all he saw was the road and the angles and the geometry of it.

She must have taken the cue because she settled back and opened her laptop. Riley was like him—work was her go-to.

It wasn't rush hour, so they made steady progress toward the safe house. Pierce kept checking his environment but so far, all clear. No one following them. Suddenly Riley gave an exclamation.

"What?"

She turned her beautiful eyes toward him in alarm. "Pierce! Does Jacob Black have a drone accompanying us?"

"I don't think so." He tapped twice, and he put the question to Black. Then turned to her. "Nope. Black says no Black Inc. drones. Why?"

"There's a drone following us. It's been with us for ten minutes. About a hundred yards behind us!"

Goddamn!

Pierce told the other two drivers. The comms would be absolutely secure in Black Inc. vehicles. They were discussing countermeasures when Riley shouted, "The drone just shot something at us! Evade!"

"Evade!" he shouted and the three vehicles scattered as an explosion hit where the middle vehicle had been just seconds before. Their vehicle was heavily sound proofed but they could feel the percussive effects nonetheless, and great clots of asphalt and dirt rained down on the hood.

"Hang on!" Pierce shouted as he wrenched the wheel and

went off-road, driving over curbs, over a grassy sward. They were on Virginia Avenue, just across from the Watergate.

He crossed traffic to get to the hotel garage. Pierce accelerated down into the parking garage, breaking the boom gate, going down two flights. He braked heavily, coming to rest an inch from the wall, exploding out the driver's door. Riley understood and was already standing beside her door, backpack on, ready to take her cues from him.

Good girl. Man, this was a woman in a million. She wasn't hysterical and she wasn't terrified and she was looking to him, ready to follow his lead.

He was ready to lead but—where? Goddamn. There was a leak somewhere. He had no idea how, but the leak had to be in Black Inc. So going back to the safehouse was out of the question. He tapped his ear piece twice.

"You guys okay? Roberts and Cullin?" The teammates in the middle. The ones targeted. "And Black, is he okay?"

"This is Roberts," came a breathless voice. "It barely missed all of us—thanks for the heads up!"

"Thank Riley. She's the one who saw it. Is the drone still operational?"

"No. Archer shot it down. But now we have to wait for law enforcement to come. Where are you?"

Pierce hesitated. He trusted these men but there was possibly a mole inside Black Inc. He felt really sorry for the poor bastard when Jacob Black found out. But in the meantime, he was responsible for Riley's safety and they had to go off grid. "Riley and I are going to disappear. I'll get in touch later."

Now it was Roberts' turn to hesitate. "Roger that. Keep her safe."

"I intend to. Out."

Pierce kept an eye on the ramp. So far, no one was coming down it. They'd be all agitated topside because of the intrusion.

He grabbed Riley's hand and headed for the elevator. "We'll have to go out through the lobby. Can you kill the cameras there?"

She was balancing her laptop on an arm. "I think I'll take all the security cams out, that way there won't be an emphasis on the lobby. And kill the ones in the elevator, too."

He wanted to kiss her. And did.

She looked startled, that delectable mouth open in surprise. He pointed at the laptop. "You done?"

She pressed another key, said, "Yes," and placed the laptop back in her backpack.

"Okay. Here are the rules for crossing the lobby. We have to look like we belong there, and we can't stand out, so no rushing. But we have to be fast. The way to do that is to lengthen your stride. We will be absorbed in each other, not noticing anyone or anything else. People pick up on attention. Hold on to my arm and try to keep up without showing effort. We'll be heading for the exit. Got that?"

"Yes. Move fast without appearing to. Act the part of a self-absorbed couple. Head for the exit."

"Good girl." She was. She grasped exactly what had to be done.

In the elevator, Pierce explained the next steps. "I hate to say this, but I think Black Inc. has somehow been compromised, otherwise they couldn't have known where we were and which vehicles to target. Which means that that nice safe house is compromised too. We can't go back there, we need to go where no one can find us."

"Where? Hotels and even Airbnbs are out. Anyone semi-competent would find us."

"I'm staying in a hotel here in DC while on ASI business. But I intended to stay over and an old friend asked me to housesit for him while he's away. I have the keys on me."

They were almost at lobby level. She turned her face up to him. "Yeah? Were you thinking of seeing the sights?"

Beautiful, brave, smart.

"No," he said on a sigh. "I was planning on introducing myself and asking you out."

Ding! The elevator doors opened.

10

I was thinking of asking you out.

Pierce dropped his bombshell just as the doors opened onto the busy lobby of the Watergate hotel. Pierce put his hand to her back and ushered her forward. She stumbled a little, her head entirely taken up with what he said.

He was going to stay on in Washington, DC to ask her out?

Oh man, that opened up an entire vista of could-have-beens that nearly stopped her in her tracks. Pierce Jordan was the most attractive man she'd ever met. And he was a good friend of her best friends. It would have been nice if he'd called, introduced himself. Asked her out for coffee. They would have enjoyed it and she'd have accepted his dinner invitation. There'd have been maybe a kiss. She would have asked him over for dinner. Another kiss, longer. They'd have spent the weekend together and have finally gone to bed together, when she knew him better.

Instead, her first glimpse of him was in a car as she was running for her life. After which he'd scared the shit out of her driving like a maniac, only it wasn't like a maniac, turned out he knew what he was doing. And ever since then, more or less every moment they'd spent together had been under a Sword of Damocles.

Except, of course, for this morning, which had been wonderful.

"Riley?" Pierce whispered.

Yeah, they were running for their lives and she was stuck like a dodo mooning over Pierce. Mooning over Pierce wasn't going to keep them alive. Constant vigilance would.

They were in the Watergate Hotel lobby, with its distinctive curved brass pillars. To the right was the famous Whiskey Bar, with its walls made of whiskey bottles. She'd spent a really boring evening there a month ago at a work function.

And right next door ...

"Follow me," she whispered to Pierce and, to his credit, he followed her unquestioningly. He must have been frantic to get going, but he was following her lead.

She walked straight into the upscale gift shop, and in a matter of seconds, she'd chosen a wide-brimmed straw hat and sunglasses for herself, a baseball cap and sunglasses for him, and paid with cash she had in her pocket, not to leave a credit card trail.

In a moment, they were crossing the lobby again, only better camouflaged. Pierce pasted a convincing smile on his face and turned to her. "Good thinking."

She nodded, smiled back. "People will remember the hats not the people wearing them."

Pierce looked like he was moving normally, but like he said, he'd lengthened his stride. She lengthened hers as well. Her legs weren't as long as his, but she managed to keep up, barely, without looking like she was running.

They looked like any other couple in the lobby—happy, carefree, dressed casually.

Pierce kept his face tilted down to her as though they were

chatting—which had the effect of shielding most of his face under the baseball cap's brim. But his eyes behind the sunglasses were constantly roaming around the immense lobby. She was sure he clocked everyone there. If they'd been followed by operators, they weren't anywhere in sight. Nobody looked remotely like an operator. Too old, too unfit, dressed wrong.

Made sense. The Watergate hotel was expensive and frequented by politically powerful people and the rich. The kind who paid other people to do things for them.

When they got to the big lobby doors, Pierce muttered, "To the right."

She followed him out, pivoted to the right with him, following a deep hedge.

Suddenly, Pierce plunged into the hedge and she followed, picking up some leaves and twigs. They came out on the other side onto some small building, an upscale mall and a big parking area.

Pierce rushed around the area, looking for something. She could see he was absorbed and said nothing, just following him. Whatever he was looking for was something that would help them and that she probably wouldn't understand.

What he was looking for, apparently, was a car to steal.

But not a new car. He gave a soft sound of satisfaction when he came upon a junker – body paint reduced to primer in places and with an old-fashioned look to it. Riley knew nothing about cars and makes and models, but even she could see that it was ancient.

And apparently, without an alarm. Pierce placed her by his side to shield what he was doing from view and in the time it would take to open the junker's driver's side door, he picked the lock. It was amazing, watching a virtuoso doing his thing.

He was already in the driver's seat when she reached the passenger seat and in the time it took her to stretch the unwieldy safety belt around her, he'd hot- wired it. The engine started up.

"Is it okay to compliment someone on his skills as a thief?" she asked. "That was really smooth."

"The Navy trained me well." His face had been tight with concentration, but he suddenly lifted his head and grinned at her, losing about ten years. He looked like a kid who had unexpectedly scored the winning basket. Then he got back that focused expressionless face.

"Hang on," he said.

Riley knew the score by then and got a good tight hold on the overhead hand grip as he pulled out of the parking spot with squealing, smoking tires, wrenching the wheel as he illegally U-turned into a busy street.

Without killing anyone.

Honestly, she had no idea how he did it.

"Here." Pierce handed her a new cell, not his. A burner. "Can you find Parker Road 132? It's in a part of town called Kalorama. Are you familiar with it?"

"Yeah. I know where it is." Riley input the address and found it immediately. "Very upscale. Very pricey. The Obamas live there. Your friend must be rich."

"He's in finance."

They were making good time, and Pierce was leaving a lot of shaking fists and impolite words behind.

"Can you take your eye off the road to look at the route or do you want me to navigate?"

"Navigate. Please."

"Okay. A right hand turn at the third street. Then straight for a mile."

She talked him to Kalorama, a mix of historical buildings, attractive new ones, bars and art galleries and upscale eateries.

"Have us stop two blocks from the address."

"Okay. Then stop … here."

He pulled in immediately into a tiny parking spot it would have taken her fifteen minutes to fit in. He turned to her. "Can you kill local security cams? Particularly all of them at Parker Road 132?"

"Sure." She pulled out her laptop, located the area, and the specific building, and killed the cams. "For how long?"

"I'd say for twenty minutes, memorize the locations and do it again when we have to come out."

She finished and looked at him. "Done. Now what?"

"Hat," he said. "Sunglasses, head down without looking furtive."

"I'll pretend to consult my cell, then."

He nodded. "Good girl."

How stupid of her to feel a rush of warmth in her chest at his words. They meant absolutely nothing. But there it was. She was flooded with feel-good hormones at two words.

He'd memorized the itinerary, but they approached the house in a great loop, his arm around her as they looked down at her switched-off cell. It wasn't any kind of hardship. Pierce was exactly the right kind of too-tall, so she fit right under his arm. He'd adjusted his stride so his steps matched hers, even though that probably meant shortening his stride. They fell into the sort of rhythm of long-time partners, and not just two people who'd only met the day before.

It was a hot day, but his body emanated even more heat than the sun. It wasn't unpleasant because she was so stressed, she was cold. Everywhere her body touched his, it warmed her up, down to her bones. She could feel absolute strength coming from him, too. From those strong muscles to the steely will in every cell of his body.

The whole package was sexy as hell. Such a distraction.

As they slithered through hedges and slinked down alleys

and dashed across lawns, all she could think about was how attracted she was. How her entire body had turned electric when they made love, sparking electricity wherever he touched her. Her mind—the thing that made her *her*, what had sustained her all her life—had been switched off, while his touch drove her crazy. Every single thing had been wildly arousing, so that when he finally slid into her, it just upped what was already an almost unbearable state of excitement. She'd come when he kissed her breasts, when his fingers entered her—and when his penis slid into her, it was more of the same, only amped to eleven.

Her legs buckled as she felt heat blast through her system. But she didn't fall, couldn't fall, because Pierce had her.

She'd lost track for a second of where they were, but he hadn't. They stopped outside a side gate surrounded by laurel bushes. On a post was written Parker Road 132, and a list of ten buzzers. "We're here," he murmured in a low voice, meeting her eyes.

She nodded as he used a code to get through the gate. There was a charming brick path surrounded by greenery, and they were at the main entrance. He used another code to get into the building and they walked straight to the bank of elevators.

Riley was finding it hard to catch her breath, anxiety like an anvil weighing down her chest. She looked up at Pierce who was totally relaxed. He bent to her. "Almost there," he murmured in her ear, tucking a lock of hair behind her ear. Two lovers, absorbed in each other, not a care in the world.

She unlocked her jaw, tried to take in a deep breath and nodded. They were the only ones in the elevator. They were in luck. It looked like the kind of building that would be full of young professionals, and they'd all still be at work at 4 pm.

They got out on the fifth floor and made their way to apartment number 502. The door required a code, and on top of that, Pierce had a key.

Riley's heart was thundering. Almost there.

The door, which was thick, opened silently and she barely got a glimpse of what looked like a nicely appointed apartment when the door swung shut with a whump, like a bank vault door.

And she was pinned against that door by a heavy, strong body. He was kissing her and kissing her and kissing her. Deep kisses, holding her so tightly it was like he was kissing her with his body, not just his mouth. After a second's surprise, Riley was with him, every step of the way.

Everything—the danger, the lies, impending war—all of it fell away. Riley could actually feel everything but Pierce just disappear, fade away from the world, and he filled her horizon. Her arms were against that strong, broad back, holding him as tightly as he held her. As if she could pull him against her so tightly she could meld with him.

She half opened her eyes to see what kind of space they were in but she just couldn't keep them open. With her eyes closed, she could focus on Pierce. On the feel of his muscles against the skin of her arms, the incredible heat his body was pumping out, his hips pressed against hers. He had a huge erection.

When had he developed that? They'd been running for their lives until two minutes ago. Evidently, though, she'd done the same thing, because she was absolutely ready for sex. As if they'd had hours of foreplay.

Some switch had been flipped, and fear had morphed into desire. Instantly. Intensely. As if hot desire were the only thing in her life and nothing else existed.

Her hands were feverishly pulling his shirt off before she even realized she was doing it. One button wouldn't work its way through the buttonhole and she just ripped it, heard it ping on the floor, and grunted when she felt his naked skin.

She felt it against her own naked skin because he'd gotten rid of the cotton sweater and cotton tank top underneath in an instant. She couldn't even remember when he did that. He slipped his big hands under her bra to cup her breasts, then just lifted her bra over her head. Nipping the skin of her neck, he unzipped his pants and let them drop, briefs, too, and they wrapped their arms around each other and swayed, chest to chest, skin to skin.

"Oh, fuck," he groaned against her lips.

There was steam in her head but she managed to ask, "What?"

He lifted his mouth from hers for a second. His mouth was red and wet and slightly swollen. Probably hers was, too.

"Pants," he whispered. "Boots."

She blinked, then understood.

She dropped to her knees, unlaced one boot then the other. She slipped them off his feet and let his pants and briefs slide off too. And looked up.

"Oh," she whispered.

Riley sat back on her haunches and simply looked her fill. He was so beautiful. A perfect man. All his muscles lean, working together. As perfect as a Greek statue. What was incredible was that he was just as perfect inside, with a big heart, a noble heart. A man who kept his word, who helped his friends, who loved his country. A man in full, a man to admire.

And he was hers.

She stood slowly, her hands covering the length of him, calves, thighs ... she took his penis in her hand. She hadn't seen many but this was just ... male perfection. She caressed him, reveling in the heat and power. She pumped once, twice, but he hissed in a breath as if in pain, and she understood he was almost overstimulated.

So was she. Her core was like a small sun and susceptible to even the slightest stimulation. If he touched her, she'd come.

Her hands travelled up, over his hard belly, chest. He stood still, watching her, almost passive. But when she put her arms around his neck, he gave a groan and brought them to the floor. They were on a rug, thick and plush, and thank God because Pierce plunged into her and started hammering at her, using the full strength of his body.

If she hadn't been so turned on, so wet, it would have hurt.

It didn't hurt.

She met him stroke for stroke, wanted the friction, wanted him as deep inside her as he could go. It was so fast and hard and intense it couldn't last, and it didn't. She was clinging to him with her arms and legs and dug her fingernails deep into the hard muscles of his back, feeling those muscles working as he moved in her. Clinging to him like a raft in a stormy sea, she went up in flames, her sex contracting around him in contractions so strong they pulled her abdominal muscles.

He gave a groan and started coming too, hips pumping, holding her so tightly she could hardly breathe. She didn't want to breathe, she wanted to be held so close to his heart, feel him moving inside her, feel his hammering heart next to her hammering heart.

They stilled, both of them. Her head was buried in his neck, her eyes closed, savoring everything.

They were both still panting. He was incredibly heavy on top of her and she was half on the cold hardwood floor, half on the plush rug. Pierce put a hand on the floor preparatory to getting up and she tightened her arms and legs around him. She was uncomfortable, yeah, but it was sheer bliss having him on top of her. She felt safe and protected, and, well—her body was still shaking from the massive orgasm. Having him in her arms was well worth a little discomfort.

He gave a little huff against her neck, lifting a lock of hair and she got goose bumps. Oh man, she was in such bad trouble. If she had more energy, she'd worry about it.

"You okay?"

Riley wiggled her toes and fingers, the only parts of her body she could move. But everything seemed functional. She couldn't really muster words. Just a humming sound and a nod of her head.

"I'm sorry. I don't usually—"

"Me neither," she choked out. This was way outside anything she recognized as Riley Behavior. Maybe some alien life form had taken her over. Or a fungus, like in *The Last of Us*.

"But I'm not really sorry," he added.

"Me neither," she repeated, and he gave a little laugh. Laughter seemed out of place, given that they had just nearly died. And the jury was still out on the world.

She snorted, which set him off in laughter. Like an out-of-control virus, it set her off too. The laughter came from deep in her belly, totally uncontrollable. She buried her face in Pierce's neck, but couldn't inhale his delicious scent because the laughter was too strong. She could barely breathe, shaking with it. Another snort, as she tried to breathe in air, and he howled. Helpless, Pierce rolled off her, pulling her with him. She was half on, half off him, feeling his muscles tighten with the laughter.

For an instant she had an out-of-body experience, and had a glimpse of them on the floor, looking down from the ceiling, whooping and shaking and it was so ridiculous she laughed even harder.

Her stomach muscles hurt, her eyes were leaking. Oh God. One hand was on his chest, the most amazing chest in the history of the world, and his large hand was over hers. She watched her hand move up and down as his chest rose and fell.

Time stopped as they laughed, and in that laughter was all the fear and anger they both felt dissipating. The world was reduced to right here, right now, as they convulsed with laughter.

It was easing. Riley could finally breathe, in and out. She wiped her eyes, looked over at Pierce. He had tears on his cheeks, too.

He slid out of her. They both had very wet groins. Pierce cupped her there and kissed her mouth. "I didn't use a condom. I'm always careful, though. I've got a clean bill of health. And I haven't had sex in a while."

She sighed. "I'm clean too, and I haven't had sex in a longer while. And it's the wrong time of month, or right time of month, however you want to look at it." She lay her hand against his cheek. They could have made a child. They hadn't. She was sure about that, but they could have.

That was a thought that would have had her in a panic with anyone else. With Pierce, it was a point in a data set. They'd had sex. They could have made her pregnant but they hadn't.

She propped her head on her hand and observed him. "Tell me, how did you know there were condoms in the nightstand back at the safe house?"

His mouth curved up. "Black told me."

She gasped. "He knew we were going to have sex? That's embarrassing!"

"Nah. Don't worry about it. He didn't know and he couldn't know. But he did see how I was looking at you and told me condoms were in the drawer. SEALs always plan for contingencies. It's part of our training."

She flopped on her back and contemplated the ceiling. "Huh."

"At the time I was thinking of a careful seduction, step by step." He tightened his grasp on her hand and brought it to his mouth, kissing the palm. "But what happened," he said, "that was weird. I don't usually jump women. The first time was pent up desire. This one here—I think we were celebrating not having died."

She smiled into his eyes. "Right?"

He brought her closer to him, kissed her forehead. "Some bodyguard I am." He kissed her cheek. "You were nearly blown up."

"I don't know. I'm alive, aren't I?"

Stealing a glance at him, his face went from smiling and relaxed to grim. "By a hair. I just found you and then I almost lost you."

"*Almost* is the operative word here. True, it was close, but close only counts in ..."

They said it together, "Horseshoes and grenades."

Pierce's mouth tightened. "Actually that *was* a grenade and it was fucking close. If you hadn't been on your laptop..."

"I was, though. But how could that drone know? There's got to be a leak somewhere."

He drew in a deep breath. "Yeah, that occurred to me, which is why we're here and not at the safe house. And the only place a mole could come from is Black Inc."

She nodded. "I hate to think that. Just hate it."

Pierce's jaws clenched. "Me, too." He looked at her, scowling, daring her to react. "It's not Jacob himself."

Her head drew back in horror. "No. Absolutely not. But ..."

"But..." he agreed.

With a sigh, Pierce stood and reached down a hand. She actually needed it because her muscles were made of rubber. This man was fabulous for her hormones but bad on her muscles. If she had to climb a wall at her gym right now, she wouldn't make it past the first handhold.

As soon as she was on her feet, Pierce put his arms around her and held her tightly. They were naked and she should have felt embarrassed or ashamed or … something. But she didn't. She only felt gratitude that he was at her side. And, well, she also felt some heat, which was absurd after an earth-shattering orgasm, but there it was.

She sighed and leaned into him. Into that long, strong body that was made to be leaned against.

Riley had never leaned on anyone in her life. Certainly not her mother, and her father made clear that a dinner was about all he was willing to commit himself to. If you'd asked her a couple of days ago, she'd have said she didn't want anyone in her life, and didn't need anyone. But that was ridiculous. She'd be freaking if she were facing all of this alone. But she wasn't freaking. She was scared, yes. Anxious, yes. But there was something about Pierce that told her that no matter how bad it got, he would be there.

It filled something cold and empty inside that she never knew was there.

Her head was against his chest, so when he spoke, she could feel the vibrations.

"Honey," he said, "we need to contact Black."

She sighed. Those vibrations were so sexy and so comforting that the words meant nothing to her.

"Hmm?"

He held her away from him, hands on her shoulders. "We need to talk to Jacob Black. We need to talk to him now and we need a better plan than what we've had so far."

The words swept away the orgasmic steam that had messed with her head. She blinked and suddenly she was there, with him. Facing a huge problem, but not alone.

He pushed a lock of her hair behind her ear. "Do you know a way to contact him without turning our cells on? I bet someone somewhere is trying to track us.

"Yeah, I know a way. And if they are half competent, they are tracking our phones." She looked down at herself, unhooked bra, pants and panties halfway across the room. "But I think that first we need to dress, don't you?"

11

I t was becoming a habit. The phone call from one of his men that Riley Robinson had slipped through their fingers once again.

Sommers had other things to think about, more important things. The contracts being thrown at his head, increasing his manpower, hiding most of his revenue abroad. He was becoming a kingmaker, a power, and he didn't have time for the video nonsense Robinson was spreading.

She had to be taken off the board and he'd taken care of it, or so he thought. Until his cell rang while he was in the middle of sending a team to Taiwan to protect the largest microchip factory in the world, a contract that was, in itself, worth several hundred million dollars.

So when he was interrupted, he knew it had to be a problem.

It was the head of the team sent to take out Riley Robinson once and for all. They'd used a drone, were following the convoy which they'd picked up outside the Pentagon. The drone was armed, fully functional. A no-brainer, goddammit.

Like fucking shooting fish in a barrel.

"Bad news, boss." Sommers felt an electric surge of rage. Bad news could only mean one thing. Riley Robinson was still breathing, still spreading her poison. He had multiple contracts rolling in, a general in his back pocket, his website blowing up with job offers, but there she was. Blocking him at every turn, with her goddamned video show, salting the earth. His earth. "She got away. They all did."

"How the fuck could you miss, with a fucking *drone?*" Ordinarily, Sommers tried to keep on friendly terms with his employees. They were sometimes asked to skirt the line, and usually sympathetic words and extra money smoothed everything over. But right now, he was fucking steaming. Teams of his men couldn't take out a fucking *girl?*

She'd had help in getting away from the NSO, some kind of driver. And then the car disappeared. A boyfriend, maybe. But everyone said she was single. So who was the man? They had no images of him.

She'd gone to ground then. She didn't go back to her apartment. He'd had his men stake it out. She didn't have any friends to stay with that he could find. She hadn't taken a plane, train, or bus out of the city. She hadn't checked into a hotel or an Airbnb. Where the fuck was she?

MacBride told him that she'd showed up at the Pentagon with Jacob Black, which was interesting. Black had always been jealous of the Sommers Group, though Black Inc. was bigger. So of course, Black would jump at anything that made his company look bad, because the Sommers Group was right up there with the big boys.

Black was helping Riley Robinson make the rounds, shilling for the bitch. Trying to tarnish the name of the Sommers Group. Of course he'd do that—he was their competitor. Sommers had no idea how he'd hooked up with the Robinson woman but Black's intelligence apparatus was first-rate. He'd heard about her, heard she was making allegations against him, and he partnered up immediately.

But Jacob Black was in for a fucking surprise.

The Sommers Group was going to overtake Black Inc., leave it in the dust. Black was essentially a nobody, had hard limits on the kind of contracts he would accept, and Sommers was going to eventually eat his fucking lunch.

However, the briefing at the Pentagon was bad, in every sense. The only good thing was that the 'evidence' shown by the Robinson bitch was highly technical, and only the lower ratings got it. The top brass didn't.

So was Black hiding her? Sommers had hired someone from Black Inc. who'd left the company on bad terms. He still had inside info, and Sommers was able to pinpoint Black as part of a convoy. With the girl.

Fuck. That was just too delicious to pass up. Sommers had acquired four drones with grenade launchers manufactured by the Chinese. Any debris picked up would be Chinese and feed the war frenzy. It was win-win. Take Black and the Robinson bitch off the chessboard and blame China.

A drone couldn't be deployed over the Pentagon but as soon as the convoy took off, he launched it.

He wanted to destroy the Robinson bitch, but wasn't it just fucking grand that he could take out Black, too? At the same time? Or at least incapacitate him.

Sommers had had every intention of following the drone, watching as it took out two problems in one stroke, but he had a prospective client in Taipei on Zoom promising to throw money at him, and he had to take it. It was a productive talk.

And then a few seconds after hanging up, realizing that the Sommers Group was going to grow into a leading security company in the world, he'd felt a wave of adrenaline course through his veins.

And then finding out Robinson and Black had evaded his fucking drone and now Sommers didn't know where Robinson was.

He put out a company-wide alert for the Robinson woman and immediately fielded an offer from Singapore for a multimillion-dollar contract. He was going to have to hire new operators. Open up another Panama account. Think of opening a Sommers Group office in Kuala Lumpur. Expand his headquarters here in DC.

Goddamn, he was going to be a king. He just needed the Robinson woman dead.

Pierce found some clothes to change into in Harrison's closet. Harrison was a clotheshorse, so Pierce had to look hard to find ordinary-looking clothes. He didn't like too-fancy stuff, plus fancy clothes drew the eye. If and when they ventured outside, they needed to look unobtrusive. Already Riley was a magnet for men's eyes, and women, too, looked on her with envy.

Pierce should be ashamed of himself. In the middle of a mission, jumping a woman like a wolverine in heat. And he *was* ashamed of himself, in some part of his head. But in the rest of him, nope. He felt *great*. Like he was on top of the world. They'd faced death and had celebrated their survival in the most ancient, most human of ways. That made total sense to him. It didn't matter that this was the first time sex had been on his mind during a mission, but then everything about this situation was an outlier. Particularly the way he felt about Riley.

But now that they'd celebrated not being dead, time to move on.

The apartment was small but luxurious. A master bedroom, a study that also had a cot for visitors, combo kitchen-dining area, one big master bath and a half bathroom. Riley went straight into the master bath and he heard the shower start up. It was one of those 'pretend you're having a shower that smells of lavender in the rain forest' deals, with six shower heads. Riley hung up her clothes on hangars, and the steam had straightened them out. She looked crisp and refreshed when she came out. When she opened the bathroom door, she looked around for him and when she saw him, she smiled. A full-on smile that lit her face. Like sunshine breaking through on a cloudy day.

Something knocked in his chest and he put a fist to his heart. It hurt.

"Hey," he said softly.

"Hey," she answered.

He started toward her but stopped at the chyron. He'd turned on the TV to a cable news channel, volume muted. Alarmed, he switched the volume on.

The usual big-haired woman with lots of teeth had a worried expression on her face.

Good afternoon, and welcome to the top news of the hour. In a recent development, tensions have escalated between China and the United States following the downing of an American MQ-1 drone, known as a Reaper drone, by a Chinese jet.

According to reports, the incident took place in the South China Sea, where the drone was conducting a routine surveillance mission. The Chinese jet reportedly intercepted the drone and shot it down, claiming that the drone had violated China's airspace and was conducting illegal spying operations.

The United States has strongly condemned the incident and has demanded the immediate return of the drone. In a statement released by the Pentagon, the United States called the act "unlawful" and "dangerous," and warned that it could lead to a further escalation of tensions in the region. Tensions are already rising due to an incident in the Democratic Republic of Congo, where soldiers of the People's

Liberation Army attacked American scientists studying a new variant of Ebola.

The Chinese government, however, has defended its actions and has accused the United States of provocative behavior in the region. In a statement released by the Chinese Foreign Ministry, the government called on the United States to "stop its illegal and provocative activities in the South China Sea" and to respect China's sovereignty and territorial integrity.

The incident comes at a time of increasing tension between China and the United States, particularly in the South China Sea, where China has been asserting its territorial claims over several disputed islands and reefs. The United States has been conducting regular surveillance missions in the region, which China has repeatedly denounced as a violation of its sovereignty.

The downing of the American drone is likely to further strain relations between the two countries, which are already at odds over a range of issues beyond the incident in Congo, including trade, human rights, and Taiwan.

That's all for now. Stay tuned for more updates on this developing story.

THEY LOOKED AT EACH OTHER.

"An MQ-1 drone costs thirty million dollars," Pierce said.

"And from what I understand, it carries Hellfire missiles, which cost upwards of $150,000 each."

"And next time, maybe the MQ-1 will have time to let off a missile and we've got the South China Sea covered in dead Chinese pilots and plane parts."

They looked at each other. So far, except for the inciting incident, no one had died. As soon as either an American or Chinese national died, things would spiral downwards very fast.

"You're right. We need to talk to Jacob Black," she said.

Pierce was torn, an unusual feeling for him. He was very clear on who was friend and who was foe in this world. But now ...

"We need to talk to him without him knowing where we are. Not that I don't trust Black, I trust him with my life, but there's a leak somewhere and it has to be from Black Inc. We don't know who it is and I'm not risking your life to find out."

"Yeah. I know a way to talk safely. Or rather, my buddies do. I'll route through them. We could be on the moon, for all Jacob Black could find out."

Pierce smiled. "Using the Queens? That's what we call them back in the office."

Riley smiled back. "The Queens? I like it." Her fingers travelled quickly over the keyboard—so quickly it looked like she wasn't touching the keys at all, but the air over the keys. Hope's pretty face showed on the screen, then Emma's equally pretty face.

"Hey," Hope said. "What's up? Are you okay? We're a little worried."

Riley looked at Pierce and he motioned for her to continue. She knew best how to explain what's up.

"We testified in front of some brass this morning, as you know," Riley said. "I'm not too sure we were getting through to them. I think we got through to the tech savvy aides who could follow, but I think the higher-ups were taking the deepfake at face value and didn't quite believe it could be fake. That's going to be a problem. And as if that isn't enough, our convoy was attacked going back to the safe house."

"*What?*" Hope and Emma said together.

"The fuck?" A deep voice intervened. Raul Martinez's face appeared between the two women. He looked angry. As he should.

Pierce put his hand on Riley's shoulder and she looked up at him. He waved a finger at the screen and she nodded. He should tell the next bit.

"We were in a three-vehicle convoy. Riley had the excellent idea of mixing the order up, and we brought up the rear. Jacob Black was in the middle vehicle. Somehow someone—and by *someone* I mean Adrian Sommers—found out about the post-briefing convoy and we were attacked."

Hope and Emma both drew in a deep breath in shock but Raul wasn't shocked. Like Pierce, he knew how the world worked.

"Riley saw on her laptop that we were being followed by a drone, and we were able to disperse just in time. Fucker shot a missile at us, aiming for the middle car of the convoy, where we were supposed to be. We took off. One of Black's operators shot it down."

Hope and Emma had their hands covering their mouths in shock. Raul didn't do shock, but he did do rage, and that's what he was expressing.

"Would that be Adrian Sommers attacking you? And attacking *Jacob Black?*"

Pierce smiled thinly. "Yeah. Big mistake. Sommers is clearly getting desperate. In trying to kill Riley he took a shot at Black and members of his crew. The thing is, we need to contact Black, but anonymously." Pierce bit his mouth, unwilling to say more.

Raul didn't have a problem with saying it out loud. "Because Black clearly has a leak in his house."

Pierce heard clattering in the background and Emma exclaimed, "I've got it!"

Raul turned his head to his fiancée, and Pierce saw the sappiest possible expression cross his face. He rarely saw that expression on his best friend's face. Raul usually turned a smiling face to the world, but Pierce knew it was mainly cynicism, as the world proved time and again to be as shitty as they knew it was. Raul was always waiting for further confirmation, which he always received.

But this? This was a *what a wonderful world* kind of smile that looked weird on his face. Unnatural.

Then Emma came into view and ... well, of course. She was amazingly beautiful—not as beautiful as Riley in his opinion, which he'd never share—and he knew she was really nice, a hard worker and madly in love with Raul. So that sappy look was justified.

She wasn't looking back at Raul lovingly, however. Not right now. Right now she was frowning at her monitor, pressed a button and turned her face to the camera. She talked to Pierce soberly, because when she was at work, she was all business.

"Pierce, I might have found the leak. I'm sending you the details on one Samuel K. Rafferty. He was a former Black Inc. operator, based in Miami, was fired from BI two months ago, the records don't say why. Being Miami, it was probably drugs. But he almost immediately joined the Sommers Group, as Keith Rafferty."

Okay. That made sense. Rafferty would have inside codes and passwords, which changed every three months, which they did at ASI, too, but three months hadn't gone by since his departure. And he'd know the addresses of safe houses, which made Pierce really glad he'd opted for his friend's apartment. No one knew where they were.

He shot a look at Riley, who understood.

"Okay, that's really good to know. I'll tell Black. Can you connect me to him in a way that is untraceable? And can you blur our background?"

Hope's head appeared and she looked a little disgruntled. "Of course," she said, frowning. As if he'd asked her to touch her nose and pat her head at the same time. The background on their screen became absolutely blank, light gray, no identifying characteristics whatsoever. Just his and Riley's faces, crisp and clear.

Hope tapped keys and then Jacob Black's face appeared—dark, long and narrow. And pissed.

He opened his mouth but Pierce beat him to it. "Good to see you're safe, sir. My friends assure me we are on an unhackable connection."

"If the Queens say it's unhackable, then it is." Black's jaw moved, clearly processing a strong emotion. "You wouldn't be seeing me at all if Riley hadn't warned us in time." He moved his head and it was as if he were in the same room as Riley, looking straight at her. "I owe you my life, Riley. I won't forget that soon."

Riley gasped. "Oh no, sir! You were nearly blown up because I insisted on changing the order of the vehicles. It was a statistical thing, but you nearly died. I would never have forgiven myself."

"Right now I'm glad neither of us died. But there are some hard truths we have to face. Jordan, where are you?"

Oh man. This was hard. Pierce braced himself. "With due respect, sir, I can't tell you that. Opsec. Because—"

"I have a mole," Black growled. Took in a deep breath, let it out. The closest thing he'd allow himself to stress relief. "Black Inc. has a mole, and it's hard even to say the words. We won't rest until we know who it is."

"We might know, actually." Emma's clear, high voice chimed in and another square opened up on the screen. Samuel Rafferty's picture appeared. "This is a man called Samuel Keith Rafferty. He worked for you briefly in your Miami office, but one of your men, one Nikolai –"

Black nodded. "Garin. One of my VPs."

"Yes. He fired Rafferty a while back. The report doesn't say why, but it being Miami, it might have something to do with drugs."

"I'll ask Nikolai."

"In the meantime, Rafferty had already been hired several days before as Keith Rafferty by the Sommers Group."

"Goddamn. He was clearly a spy in our house. Before he was fired by Nikolai, he'd know or have access to the lot. To the tags of our vehicles, our major passwords, our operators."

"And where your safe houses are," Pierce said.

There was total silence. Pierce knew that Black would institute a complete overhaul of his vehicles and safe house system, a monumental task. But in the meantime, any Black Inc. safe house was now ... unsafe.

"We're someplace safe now," Pierce added.

"Don't tell me," Black said urgently, holding his hand up, palm out.

"No, sir." Pierce was sad. The idea of not trusting Black and Black Inc. hurt. "I won't."

Another silence.

"Okay," Black said. "You guys sit tight. Riley's done what she could, which was amazing. But I'm not exposing her again. Now I need to contact some more people, start gaining a consensus. Start planning payback."

Against the Sommers Group. He didn't need to say it.

"Sir?" Riley barely stopped herself from raising her hand, permission to speak. She didn't need anyone's permission.

"Jacob," Black growled.

"Jacob. Yes." She stopped, swallowed. "When we were in the briefing room, I got the impression that General MacBride wasn't following the technicalities, and if you don't, it's easy to be fooled."

"MacBride is an ass. And is where he is because of politics. Guy hasn't spent time in the field in decades."

"Yessir. Um, Jacob. But General MacBride's aide, the Captain, he wasn't fooled. He followed perfectly. Contact him and have him with you, if he'll volunteer. If you guys have any difficulties, let the Queens know and they'll put me in contact with you."

"Done. I'll send the Queens briefings that they'll send to you and we can talk tomorrow. There's some kind of drumbeat for war, and we need to stop it in its tracks."

"We do," Pierce said. Anyone who had been to war—and he and Jacob Black had seen far too much of it—wanted to stop this rush to war based on a lie. It had been bad enough with weaker militaries, like in Afghanistan and Iraq. Against a very powerful enemy, in some respects more powerful than the US, war could destroy the world. "The drumbeat will be about money. Follow the money."

"Yeah. Someone's got an economic interest, and if the world burns to ashes he won't care. Probably got a bolt hole somewhere. Okay. So you'll be getting updates via ASI, and if there's another attack, I'll let you know immediately." His dark face tightened. "But it's Riley they are after, not me. When briefing, I'll make it clear that Riley's intel is out in the open and everyone should call off the dogs. She's done enough. But in the meantime, you keep her safe, Pierce."

Black's eyes seemed to bore a hole in his.

God, yes. "I have every intention of doing so, sir."

"Black, out." And his section of the monitor went blank.

Both Riley and Pierce let out a breath. They looked at each other and grinned.

"Quite a commanding personality," Riley said.

"Yeah. I'm glad he's on the side of the good guys. I'd hate to have him after me."

"Uh, guys?" Hope's soft voice interrupted. They turned back to the screen. "I'm reading from Summer that the USS *Carl Vinson* is in the Strait of Taiwan and has just sent up six F/A-18 Super Hornet fighter jets, protecting other Reaper drones. That's not good news."

"No, it isn't," Pierce agreed. This thing was escalating. Super Hornets were beasts. They had an internal 20-mm M61A2 rotary cannon, and carried air-to-air missiles, air-to-surface missiles, and other weapons. They could refuel in-flight, and could stay in the air as long as the pilots could stay awake.

Riley leaned forward. "Is that Summer Redding? Is she starting her political blog Area8 up again?"

Hope smiled. "Summer Redding-Delvaux. And yes, she's putting out her political blog again, once she heard from us what's going on. She has amazing resources, too, and she'll do a really good job."

"I know she will. Tell her to contact me if she needs any technical consultation."

"Will do."

"And how's Felicity?"

Hope grinned, and Pierce could see Emma grin at the edges of the screen. "About ready to pop from what Metal calls the longest pregnancy in history, or at least that's what it feels like, he said."

No shit. Metal's wonderful and super-smart wife Felicity was still barfing her way through her pregnancy with twin boys. Everyone felt sorry for her, nobody could do anything, and trying to make it easier for her didn't work because she always wanted to do her share of work, and more. She never ever complained. Metal had aged ten years over the course of the pregnancy. Everyone was hoping the boys would pop soon and put him out of his misery.

Those kids would be born into the ASI family and would grow up with a billion loving aunts and uncles.

Lucky kids. Pierce's family in the States was small, but he came from a huge clan back in Ireland. When he went back to visit family in County Cork, a small army of munchkins hurled themselves at him as soon as he walked through the door, wanting to be thrown in the air.

He loved it.

"Keep us updated," he said to the Queens and closed the connection.

Pierce looked at Riley, who seemed really happy for Felicity and for her friends. Not once had she mentioned family. Emma had said she was alone in the world, which seemed strange for such a beautiful woman. Not only was she beautiful, but she also seemed to lack all the toxic hallmarks of beautiful women that made them so difficult. She wasn't difficult at all. In mortal danger, she hadn't thrown a fit or even had a mood. At all times, she tried to be helpful, a characteristic she shared with the Queens.

No family, though.

No boyfriend, either.

That baffled him, too. How some guy hadn't snatched her up and not let go was beyond his comprehension.

She'd been through hell. Well. Time to try to take care of her, since no one else was going to.

Pierce suddenly found himself *wanting* to take care of her. Make her feel better. Above all, make her feel safe. If anyone wanted to hurt her, they'd have to go through him to get to her. He knew Jacob Black would be looking after her, too, and his company, but he felt that she was *his* to care for. Not a job, not a chore, not a responsibility, but a privilege.

His.

She was at the living room desk, head propped up on one hand, checking something. Right now she needed to have her head taken up with other things. Not by murder and lies and war.

He put a hand on her shoulder, feeling the delicate bones.

"Hey," he said softly, placing a black credit card on the

Swedish design desk. "We don't know how long this is going to take and you had to leave everything behind. Twice. Take this card and order some clothes. Lots of them. Anything you want. Cashmere, silk. Armani, Dior. Whatever. Everything, from the skin out. And get yourself all the toiletries you'll need, or whatever else you want. Spend lavishly."

She looked up at him curiously and checked the credit card, in the name of Hugo da Silva. "Who is Hugo da Silva?"

"No one." He grinned just thinking of it. "ASI was hired to take down a cartel and it turned out there was a huge secret bank account that the government couldn't take over because they didn't have the password, and they didn't want it anyway. The guy who hired us wanted the win, but not the paperwork to take over the account. So he said, *If you guys can crack the code, it's all yours*. Well, our Queens cracked the code in a couple of hours, and Midnight and the Senior had credit cards made out in fictitious names, for us to use in the field when we need something but have to hide our identity. We're encouraged to use them. The Queens got a new car each, and let me tell you, our chief gearhead, Jacko, was disgusted when they all wanted a Prius. Long story short, that credit card is completely anonymous and basically bottomless, so go to town."

She smiled. "Well, that's quite a story. I'll order clothes and … things, but be forewarned, my tastes run more to Lululemon than Armani, and to cotton rather than silk and cashmere."

He gently squeezed her shoulder. "Anything you want," he repeated. "And plan for a while. Have them delivered to this address. My friend's name is Harrison March. There's a doorman who will take delivery. In the meantime, my friend's a foodie and he said his freezer is full and to use whatever I wanted. Any preferences for food?" He grinned. "I remember you're not a vegetarian or a vegan."

"God no." Riley laughed. "I love meat. Not too wild about fish though. And after playing *The Last of Us*, I'm off mushrooms."

Ah. A woman after his own heart. "Gotcha. No fish, mushroom-free. You go order up a storm and I'll have dinner on the table by the time you finish."

"You a good cook?"

"You don't have to sound surprised. I grew up in an Irish household where a pot roast was a small, black, charred thing, and my ma, bless her, put the vegetables on to boil before going to mass. I learned to cook out of self-defense, though in this case, it'll be simply nuking stuff from Harrison's freezer. Do you cook?"

"Not really. I can defrost and am an ace at ordering. I can do breakfasts though."

"Good to know. So I'll leave you to it. Again, order anything you want, in quantity."

"What about you?"

"I'm more or less Harrison's size so I'll just use his clothes. He won't mind. I'll try not to get shot and put holes in the clothes. His stuff tends to be expensive."

Riley leaned back and looked around the apartment. It was super modern, decorated expensively. The master bathroom was larger than many people's living rooms, with a hot tub. The whole place screamed money and expensive decorators.

"Your friend ..."

"Harrison?"

"Yeah. What does he do for a living? Rob banks?"

Pierce smiled. "Sort of. He's a hedge fund something, and uses money to make money. It's all sort of vague. He explains it to me, but it goes in one ear and out the other."

"Emma used to work for people like that in San Francisco. She said they were all disturbed, soulless people."

Pierce sighed. "I met Harrison in college, we were roommates. He's sure not disturbed or soulless, but he does have a hard-on for money. He was on a scholarship and never talked about his family, but I gather he had a hard time of it. Harrison's gay, and I think his family is super religious and didn't approve, to put it mildly. They also didn't approve of music, TV, and movies. And their approved reading list was basically the Bible. So Harrison is hell-bent on making money and having fun and more power to him."

"Okay. Well, good for him. And it looks like he's done well for himself. I personally am not really that interested in money. You should, um, know that. Once I have the basics, I'm more interested in challenging work than in work that pays super well. Like I said, I have plain tastes, except in food, entertainment and people."

"Well, we're on the same page there. ASI pays really well, we have absolutely no complaints. But we're not in it for the money, and all of us feel really loyal to the company, and the heads are loyal to us. Unlike—"

Pierce's mouth pinched shut.

Riley waited him out.

Goddamn, Pierce hated even saying it. "Unlike the military."

His jaw locked. It still hurt like shit. The Navy hadn't stood by them at all. Had thrown them to the wolves when they reported the murdering psychopath commander who loved shooting civilians.

So very unlike the heads of ASI, two honorable men, John Huntington and Douglas Kowalski. Loyal to the bone.

It had been clear to Raul and him that their military careers were over. They'd both retired from the Navy and ASI had snapped them up.

ASI was much more loyal to its people than the Navy had been.

Riley put her hand over his, snapping him out of his memories.

"I'm so sorry," she said softly. "That shouldn't have happened to you."

Her hand was as beautiful as the rest of her—pale and slender and finely shaped. He could feel her touch all the way up his arm. He was getting a semi-woodie, and now was not the right time for it.

He leaned forward, planted a kiss on her forehead and moved off. "So I'll see to the food and you get yourself kitted out. See you in the kitchen in half an hour."

She looked up and smiled. "Don't forget dessert."

12

C lothes shopping was surprisingly tedious and boring, even when you could buy whatever you wanted. Or at least Riley got bored in twenty minutes. She knew exactly what she wanted and where to buy it.

Ten of her favorite brand of yoga pants, four pairs of slacks, all exactly like the ones she had at home. Five cotton sweaters, all alike but in different colors, five tank tops, a couple of cotton cardigans, five hoodies, a raincoat, underwear of the plain cotton variety, three light cotton PJs, socks, two pairs of flats, two pairs of boots, two pairs of sneakers. Her favorite brands of shampoo and conditioner, a good day cream, a good night cream, lipstick, eye liner. A roll-on bag in a dull, nondescript shade of gray.

And then her shopping energy sputtered.

There was a pretty summer dress that gave her pause, and she had hovered over it with her cursor but ... nah. Where would she wear it? She didn't wear dresses normally, and on the run? Who wore a dress when they were on the run?

Though it was very pretty ...

Everyone promised that everything would be delivered by the end of the business day. So that was that.

Pierce had given her half an hour, so she politely waited until the half hour had gone by and then walked into the dining room.

Pierce was setting the table and looked up, surprised. "Finished so soon?"

She was surprised, too. "You said half an hour. It's been half an hour. Exactly."

"I was expecting you to take hours." He shook his head. "Do you know how much you spent?"

"To the penny, actually. $1,850.38." All of a sudden, she was anxious. "Is that too much? You did say no limits."

Pierce gave a crack of laughter. He came around the table, kissed her hair and sat her down on one of the chairs. "I once dated a model who would have spent double that on a handbag and if I'd said 'go to town,' she'd have done just that and spent a hundred grand or more. Did you get enough stuff? If you forgot anything, don't worry, that credit card isn't going anywhere."

"We're sort of living on the edge, right? On the run. I figured I'd need low maintenance stuff and not too much of it. So what's all this?"

The table was covered with food, steaming and smelling delicious. She was famished. The last meal had been almost twenty-four hours ago, and a lot had happened in the meantime. Harrison had an amazing collection of serving plates—colorful Fiestaware that she knew cost a fortune. The plates were heaped. The plates themselves were colorful, the food was colorful, and it was a delight for all the senses. And a real contrast to her usual meals, particularly over the past days as she puzzled out the video that had come in.

Her food was usually as bland-looking as her plates, all mismatched because it had been easier to rent a furnished apartment, and her landlord had furnished it with castoffs. Lunch was in the canteen and dinner meals were ramen or yogurt or oatmeal or tired-looking salads that came in a bag. Half the time, she wasn't even aware of what she was eating.

This was nothing like that. This was life itself, color and variety served by the best-looking man she'd ever seen. She was on the run, but life was definitely looking up.

Her stomach, which had been closed, suddenly opened up. *Yawned* open, in fact. She was ravenously hungry and had an appetite for everything. Yes, she was on the run and war loomed. But that was all outside the door of this ridiculously expensive apartment. It was as if her life had been this dreary indie movie and all of a sudden it became a Bollywood extravaganza.

"Harrison is amazing." Pierce elected to sit next to her and started loading a plate for her. "Let me know if you don't like something."

"So far, everything looks delicious. Amazing how?"

"Well, he's super organized, for one. I'm organized, but mostly about my gear, definitely not my food. He has two freezers and a list of everything in them, the date he froze it, and if it came from a restaurant, which one. And they are organized by type of food. Meat, fish, pasta, and rice dishes, breads, vegetables, sweets. Totally OCD, but it makes it easy to put together a meal."

"A feast, you mean," Riley said, looking over the table and then at her plate. "So what do we have here? Chicken breasts and…"

Pierce pointed out the items. "Linguine al pesto, chicken breasts Marsala, sweet potato matchstick fries, a slice of eggplant parmesan, slice of zucchini frittata, rosemary rice balls and sourdough garlic bread. He has a lot of cuisines, but I chose mainly Italian because you liked Italian yesterday, and anyway you can't go wrong with Italian food. Right?"

Riley nodded enthusiastically. She couldn't speak because

her mouth was full of pasta. Delicious. She pointed at Pierce's plate and made a questioning sound.

"What's this, you're asking? Pumpkin risotto. To die for. Here." He held out a forkful of fragrant yellow rice and brought it to her mouth. She swallowed her pasta and opened her mouth and he tipped it in perfectly. Oh, man. So delicate and tasty.

"You're good at spooning food in people's mouths."

His rolled his eyes. "I should be, considering I have twenty-two nieces and nephews and I've fed every single one of them. Messy little beasts." He grinned.

Riley's jaw dropped. "Twenty-two nieces and nephews? How do you keep them all straight? And how many siblings do you have?"

"Easily enough, and only two, Moira and Brendan. But I have a lot of cousins, and I consider their children like the kids of siblings. Each little rug rat has his or her own personality on steroids, so it's not hard to remember their names, believe me." He narrowed his eyes at her. "You have no nieces or nephews?"

"No." Riley averted her eyes. In the world she lived in, families were never a factor. Didn't even exist, everyone was like a solitary molecule in space. She had no idea if any of her colleagues had siblings, or even parents. They could all have been hatched from eggs, as far as she knew. It was only when she went out into the world that she realized how strange her own world was.

"Parents?"

Oh God. Pierce was insisting. This is where she usually lied, changed the subject or broke it off. Went somewhere else. But there was nowhere for her to go. She was tied to Pierce, but beyond that, she didn't want to lie to him or break off something great that had just begun.

Bite the bullet. The only thing she could do.

"Okay, um. Full disclosure. I come from a dysfunctional

background, though I'm not dysfunctional myself. Or, at least I don't think I am. My mom was a wild child, got into drugs and alcohol early and never really got out. I was brought up by my grandmother, who also left me a small inheritance. Enough for me to study without worrying too much, and I had scholarships. She died when I was eighteen. My mom died while I was on a study program in Paris. No one told me because they didn't know she had a daughter. She'd been dead for six months before I found out."

She watched him as she talked. The few people she'd told had cycled through the whole range of emotions—horror, pity, pain. Pierce kept his expression neutral, but his eyes were warm, as were his hands as he took her hands in his.

"I'm really sorry that happened to you. What about your father?"

She sighed. "That's another sad tale. My mother got pregnant from a one- night stand. She was in one of her rare sober periods and lived with her mother, my grandmother, who kept a close eye on her. My grandmother finally told me his name, and so I contacted him. A lawyer who lived on the West Coast, near Los Angeles. I called him. He seemed friendly enough, and I flew out to meet him. I remember—" She closed her eyes and for the very first time smiled at the memory. "I remember being so very excited. Family. I was going to find my family. I researched him and he'd been a musician before going to law school in his late twenties. He was a fairly well-known lawyer. At the time it seemed the most stable, desirable job in the world, and just the idea made me feel ... safe I guess." She huffed a laugh. "I must have been the only person in the world who felt safe with a lawyer."

He was watching her carefully, listening to her carefully, soaking up her story through every sense. Through touching her, too, his hands warm and strong.

"He met me at the airport, took me out to dinner at a nice place." Riley stopped, remembering that evening so very clearly. The electric excitement, the feeling of having turned a page, of entering into the human family with a family of her own. The nice restaurant, her gratitude that her grandmother had insisted on table etiquette so she knew she wasn't embarrassing herself. The light chitchat. Her father had steered way clear of talking about anything emotional. He didn't blink when Riley told him her mother had passed away. "When we finished dinner, he drove me to my hotel. I was waiting for him to mention an appointment for the next day. Crazily, in my head, I was exploring my options for moving out West. I had a number of scholarship offers, including UC Berkley. I could have and definitely would have transferred to California to be near my only family member. He leaned over, kissed my forehead and said he couldn't drive me to the airport the next day because he had an important business meeting and was leaving for a work trip to Seattle the day after."

Riley probed the memory, like you probe a sore tooth. It had taken years before she could think about that evening without a sharp spasm of unbearable pain. She probed again but the intense pain was gone. It was like recalling a long-ago car accident.

"Let me guess," Pierce said. "He wasn't interested in continuing the relationship."

"That's putting it mildly. He was astonished that I thought he would care. When I said—I said I could wait for him to return, he just looked at me blankly and said, *Why would you do that*? He drove off and I haven't seen or heard from him since."

Pierce sighed.

"It's okay." Those were rote words, but Riley was astounded as she said them, to realize that they were true. It *was* okay. Ten years had passed, ten years in which she had been immersed in her studies and had had a couple of demanding, fulfilling jobs. It felt like a lifetime ago and in one sense, it was. She was an entirely different person from the scared, needy young girl she'd been.

Her 'father' had missed out on her. His loss. She'd have been a loyal and loving daughter. But he didn't want her and that was that. She'd gone on to have a life, a good one.

"What an asshole," Pierce mused and Riley snorted a laugh.

"Yeah, you're right. He is an asshole. But I'm not alone in the unlucky genetics department. Hope's grandfather tried to have her killed. Hard to beat that. Families are hell."

Hope's grandfather, a powerful man, hadn't approved of his son's love affair with Hope's mother, and had arranged an accident that killed her mother and put Hope in a coma.

"Mostly, yeah. Mine isn't. My parents are teachers and my sister is a teacher and my brother is a biologist, and they're good people and we get on really well. I only ever fought once with my parents, when I announced I was joining the Navy. Nobody in my family has ever even held a gun in their hands. Everyone expected I'd become a teacher too, but the sad fact is that I wasn't academically inclined." He grinned. "What I really wanted to do was blow shit up. Being in the military was not what they envisaged for me. My mom wouldn't speak to me for a week. That really hurt."

"Well, you're not in the military anymore."

"No, but I work for a security company and carry a gun. We avoid talking about it."

Riley looked at him, at that handsome face behind which was a good soul. Those broad shoulders that took on the burdens of others, those big capable hands she entrusted with her life. "I'm glad you do. I wouldn't be here otherwise."

And leaned forward to kiss him.

13

Pierce let himself be kissed. A soft, gentle *thank you* kiss. It helped, because while eating, he'd been so turned on he was glad the table hid his woodie. It had subsided while she told the story of her family, a real downer.

Well no downers now, only things that made him go up.

The kiss was a start.

He dug his fingers in her hair, soft and fragrant, cupping her head. Deepened the kiss. He ran a finger along her neck and felt her gasp.

Oh, now that was interesting.

Pierce lifted his head. "You know, we've gone so fast I haven't had a chance to map your erogenous zones. I was really good at map reading during training."

She lifted heavy eyelids. Those eyes were so amazing. Long, dark eyelashes framing eyes like a glowing dawn, filled with light. A smile. "You were?"

"Mmm." Holding her head still, he rose, and she rose with him. He kissed her, deep and long. Opened an eye and measured the distance to the master bedroom, walking with a *hard* hard on. The door to the bedroom looked miles away and he wasn't going to make it.

But! He was a former Navy SEAL and nothing was too hard, no mission too impossible. He could make it to the bedroom if he tried really hard.

Trying really hard was the essence of being a SEAL.

Step by step.

He made it to the living room rug. One of those plush Chinese deals that were as soft as a mattress. That was really tempting because kissing Riley was making him so hot it was embarrassing. He was hard as a rock.

Riley licked his tongue and, for a second, he thought he was going to come in his pants. Really embarrassing. He was known for his self-control. He hadn't come in his pants since fucking high school. She licked inside his mouth again and an electric streak ran from his backbone to his balls and oh God. No.

Pierce tightened his ass and thought *fuck this*, and swung her up in his arms. She was going to interpret it as a romantic gesture, and only he knew it was so he wouldn't shame himself in Harrison's living room.

When he swung her up, she made a small noise of surprise, then melted in his arms.

Pierce made it to the edge of the bedroom, which was valiant, braced himself, and made it to the bed, which was heroic. Couldn't believe he'd made it. He sank down with Riley in his arms. She felt so good, like she was made to be there. Slender, supple, soft.

And now his brain split in two. One part really liked lying here on that big comfortable bed, holding Riley in his arms. The other part wanted to take her, hard and fast.

Maybe he could try self-control for a change.

He pressed small, biting kisses all over her face, speaking between kisses. "You know, mapping a terrain is tricky."

"Mmm?" she smiled, making a questioning noise. Her eyes were closed, and she stretched out under him like a cat. She liked having her face kissed. Good to know.

Neck?

"Going to map your body." Pierce ran tongue and teeth along the long, slim neck and bingo! She drew in a breath and shuddered slightly. "This area works," he whispered as he bit, then licked the spot. He knew his five o'clock shadow would be tickling her, too.

He brought his mouth down, down until he nuzzled her breast. She had the most beautiful breasts he'd ever seen. Firm and pale, with light pink nipples. He licked and suckled and then bit her lightly, making her jump. "Breasts, check."

"I think it'll be hard to find a part of my body that isn't an erogenous zone," she said lazily. "Who knew?"

"You didn't know?"

Riley laced her fingers on his chest and rested her chin on them. "To tell you the truth, before you, I'd have said I have one erogenous zone. Two, tops. But right now, I think where I have skin, if you touch it, it turns me on. I don't think you need to map anything. You touch me anywhere, and that works."

His whole chest filled with heat. "That's really good to know. But I am a believer in the scientific method. Test all theories. That's what I was taught."

She smiled. "You know I was trained in math and physics so I follow the scientific method, too."

"Yeah?"

"Yeah."

Watching her eyes, he circled her nipple and watched it rise, harden, turn red.

Riley did the same to his nipple. Circled it with her finger, watched it rise and harden. His dick was already up and hard.

She leaned over and licked his nipple and it was a line straight to his dick. It moved, lengthened a little.

"That's interesting." Riley's voice had turned low, incredibly sexy. "What else makes it move?"

"Why don't you find out?"

She ran her hand over his belly, watching his dick twitch. He ran a hand down her pale flat belly, watching her eyes.

"You know," he said, "women have a great advantage. You can literally tell with a guy if something turns him on. It's visible, tangible."

Riley closed her fist around his dick and he hissed. He felt like he was going to explode.

"But with women, it's more subtle. Hidden. But it is possible to know what's going on, if you know where to look."

Pierce covered her sex and waggled his hand so she'd spread her legs. She lifted them, spread them. Her legs, too, were the most beautiful legs he'd ever seen. A runner's legs—long, slim, strong. The sight of his hand between her legs was incredibly erotic, like he'd staked his claim.

And he had.

"So let's see what's happened here, hmmm?" Pierce circled the opening to her sex. It was wet. He penetrated her with his finger, the soft tissues closing around him. "Looks like you were turned on, too."

"Pierce." Her face had lost that look of amusement. It was serious now, mouth slightly open as if to take in more oxygen. "Now, Pierce."

Yes, now.

He held her open with his fingers as he entered her. They both sighed at the same time, that feeling of something right, of something meant to be, hitting them both. He could feel it in her kisses, in her skin, in her heart, of something momentous happening. Something right.

Something big.

RILEY DRIFTED UP TOWARD CONSCIOUSNESS, like slowly rising up through the sea after a dive. Up, lazily up, toward the light. But it was quite pleasant here, too.

Here, right now, meant lying on a warm, hard body, like lying on hard compacted sand that had soaked up the rays of the sun. It was as if she'd been on vacation in some impossibly attractive place like Bali or Sicily. Muscles lax, heat penetrating her bones.

Happy and relaxed.

A big hand cupped her head, fingers slowly massaging her scalp, and yes, that was part of the fantasy. Because if she was in Bali, of course there had to be a giant hand giving her a head massage. That's how fantasies worked.

Then his stomach rumbled. And then hers.

And she snapped completely awake, oriented in time and space. She knew exactly where she was and with whom. She was in Harrison Whosis' apartment and with Pierce Jordan, the man who'd loved her into a stupor last night.

And just like that, for the very first time in her life, reality was better than fantasy.

His stomach growled again. He laughed. "Good morning." His voice was a rough rumble, like the giant's voice in a fairy tale.

"Morning," she sighed, eyes closed. Morning was not good. Morning meant the day starting, meant reality rushing in. During the nighttime, in the darkness, they could pretend they were two lovers on some desert island, cut off from the rest of the world. But the rest of the world came rushing back in crushing waves, heavy and dark and dangerous.

She opened her eyes to find Pierce's deep blue eyes staring into her own.

The few times she had slept over with a lover, the next morning was inevitably awkward. Up until now, Riley had specialized in semi-autistic, socially inept men, and the morning after the night before was always painful. The whole morning routine—showering, getting dressed while trying to preserve some modesty though they'd both been naked all night, grabbing some breakfast—was always awkward.

Riley didn't feel awkward now. She felt *great*.

Pierce smiled at her and she smiled right back. He ran a hand up her arm, cupped her shoulder, kissed her. Then he threw back the covers and stood up and oh my God. His muscles had muscles. He looked like the David by Michelangelo, only better endowed.

"You should never get dressed," she said seriously.

Pierce laughed.

"I mean it. You should just go around naked, make everyone's day."

She was lying on her side, the covers pooled around her feet.

He gave her a slow appreciative glance, head to feet and back again. "I'd say the same thing, but trust me when I say I don't want anyone but me seeing you like this. My very own work of art, which only I get to see."

"Only you," Riley agreed, smiling. Right now she couldn't remember a thing about any of the few men she'd gone to bed with, except that they all paled in comparison with Pierce.

"No." Pierce had lost his smile. "I really mean it." He waved a long finger between them. "Whatever this is, what we have between us, I want it to be exclusive."

He said it almost belligerently, feet widened in a boxer's stance, as if she were going to beat him up for saying it.

She wasn't going to beat him up. He didn't have to convince her. She couldn't even imagine being with anyone else.

"Oh yeah," she breathed.

He perked up. "Yeah?"

"Well, if you can put up with me."

"Put up with you?" He sounded puzzled. "You're perfect."

Riley gave a very unladylike snort of laughter. The men she'd dated would have begged to differ. "Not quite. I get lost in my work. I can't cook. I—"

"Stop it." Pierce was shaking his head. "Speaking of cooking, I'm going to go deal with breakfast. I told you Harrison has a whole section labelled 'Breakfast'. I think there might be croissants. And muffins." He bent and kissed her neck, smiling as he rose because she shivered. "That neck is definitely an erogenous zone."

It had felt like an electric shock. "Mmm."

"Hold that thought." He dressed in jeans and a tee, and all Riley could think about was how sad it was that he covered that body up. But at some point, they were going to have to go out, she supposed, and he'd stop traffic—at least vehicles driven by women—if he went around naked.

She took a shower, marveling at herself. Showers were quick and efficient ways to get clean. Unless she was washing her hair, her morning shower took between five and eight minutes. She'd timed it when she started taking the bus to work. But now? She stood dreamily under the cascade of hot water, remembering last night and she could have stayed forever. Soaping up, she remembered Pierce touching her, all over. How his rough hands had been so gentle, how she'd shivered yet had been so hot.

If they lived together, she'd never get out of bed.

Riley froze, sponge in hand. *If they lived together.* Man, was she getting ahead of herself. So far, they were having an affair. A hot affair, true, but an affair. Earlier, he had said he wanted it to be an exclusive relationship which was fine because she couldn't imagine being with another man. But there was a lot of road to travel between a hot affair with a man she'd just met and living together. She couldn't be all starry-eyed. It wasn't fair to him and wasn't fair to her.

Take it one step at a time, she told herself sternly.

She'd learned at a very young age that yearning for something and getting it were two entirely different things.

She talked sense into herself while she toweled dry and dressed in one of the cotton sports outfits she'd bought, light blue in color. Maybe, when this was over and they were still standing, she'd branch out from sportswear.

Maybe, when this was all over, if she was still alive and they were still together, she'd buy herself some dresses. Shoes not sneakers. A proper handbag and not a backpack. Dress up instead of down.

If she survived the next little while, having a lover put a whole new perspective on things. Going to the movies and concerts with someone. Company on weekends.

Sex on tap.

Oh God, yes.

The future stretched deliciously in front of her. True, they lived on opposite coasts, but it was possible that she'd lose her job at the NSO. Probable, even. She hadn't done anything wrong, but her name was tainted now. She'd become a political hot potato in a political city. Maybe—maybe she'd move out West. Maybe—maybe even to Portland. Her best friends lived there, after all. She had no doubt she'd find a job, a good one. Work had never been a problem. And she had considerable savings so she could even afford to take her time.

She walked into the dining room smiling, happy with everything, including the spread on the table. Everything that made for a luscious breakfast was there, including both tea and coffee.

Croissants, yes, and muffins, yes. Wholewheat toast, a couple of types of jam, an expensive brand of imported salted butter. Boiled eggs in pretty egg cups. Greek yogurt, muesli, hot waffles and hot syrup. It was more breakfast food than she ate in a week.

"I boiled the eggs myself," Pierce said proudly, seating her, unfolding a massive linen napkin and placing it on her lap, then sitting down himself. "I timed it. Four minutes. That okay?"

He could have boiled the eggs for twenty-four hours for all she cared. "Fine."

His hand hovered over the coffee pot and tea pot. "Tea or coffee? He had one of my favorite teas, Lady Grey."

"Sure. I love tea, and particularly Lady Grey. And then after, I'll have a cup of coffee, too, wake me right up."

"Great." He beamed and kissed her cheek. "Tea coming right up."

"Someone's in a good mood."

"I know." He winked. "I'm not usually in a good mood in the morning, but I had a fantastic night. And I feel great."

She put down her croissant and turned to face him. "You know, me too. I feel great. I'm not usually cheerful in the morning, either."

"Here. Have some carbs and cholesterol." He thrust a muffin at her, slathered with butter and took her hand. He turned serious. "You know, I think we have something here and—"

They were interrupted by the particular sounds of the HER room coming from Riley's laptop, and they both sobered, instantly. The ugly mug of the Goblin King filled the screen.

They'd been living for a few hours in a little cocoon, safe and sound. And the world was intruding again. The world had fangs and claws and was full of bad things. It drew blood.

Riley pushed away her plate and reached over for her laptop, all hunger gone.

She looked over at Pierce, a last lingering look, like the last rays of sunshine before darkness descended. She wanted to capture this moment, keep it, but it was like trying to catch the rays of the sun.

The HER room was rarely used for good news.

She clicked on and saw Hope's face. "Riley, sorry to interrupt, but I've got Jacob Black on the line and he wants to talk to you and Pierce."

It was sad to acknowledge that they couldn't talk to Jacob Black directly. It was direct testimony to how fucked up this situation was.

"Go," she said, and Jacob Black's narrow, grim face filled the screen.

"Riley. Is Pierce with you?"

"Yessir. Jacob." She shifted and Pierce moved his chair so that he was in the view of the laptop's camera.

"Sir." Pierce's entire body language had shifted, as had hers. No longer relaxed, loose. He was sitting, but at attention. She was sitting, too, straight and stiff. "Sitrep?"

Jacob sighed. "Not good, Jordan. I've had back-to-back meetings, and I've got General Carville and Colonel Navarro on my side. Not to mention some Army techs who know what they're doing. But we're beating our heads against a couple of walls. First of all, brass that doesn't understand the tech and thinks that we're blowing smoke out our asses and secondly—" He looked away for a second, jaws clenched tight. Riley was scared for a moment because he looked frightening. He was a dangerous man.

But he was a dangerous man on their side, so she kept her expression neutral. But there was no doubt that he was enraged. "There are some who are happy, and they are being encouraged by Adrian Sommers, who has several contracts in the bag. He's built up assets in the East, and he's spoiling for a fight. These assholes are convinced we can keep conflict from scaling up, while degrading China's military. It's crazy. We're talking the Cuban Missile Crisis on steroids, and there is a good chance this will blow up into a shooting war, very soon. Even nuclear capability is not off the table."

Riley turned, appalled, to Pierce. Everyone's worst nightmare. Nuclear warfare. But apparently not everyone's worst nightmare.

"No one wins a nuclear exchange," Pierce said soberly.

Black's jaws clenched as if he were chewing something bitter. "Tell that to the decision-makers who have never been to war. For them it's blips on a computer screen. Not dead men, women and children."

Riley saw Jacob Black and Pierce exchange hard looks through the screens. Both of them knew all too well what war meant.

"There's more." Black's eyes narrowed.

"More than possible war with a nuclear power?" Riley asked.

He blew out a breath. "They're saying that your proof has been reverse engineered. It's quickly becoming the accepted narrative."

Riley sat back, hoping against hope she misunderstood. "What?"

"Yes. They are saying that you took the original video of Chinese troops attacking American scientists and clumsily tried to turn it into a fake video, casting blame on the blameless operators of the Sommers Group. As a cover-up. Paid for by the Chinese."

Her heart began to hammer. "That would be treason. Sir."

Jacob Black's head bowed. "It would be, indeed. Punishable by imprisonment for life. If it goes to a shooting war, punishable by death."

"Hey!" Next to her Pierce bristled. "What the fuck? That's ridiculous, no one who knows Riley—"

She held up a finger and Pierce stopped midsentence.

"There would be the time stamps," she said evenly. "Showing Sommers Group operators and *then* the Chinese."

"They're going to say that if you can create a deepfake, you can fake the time stamps, too."

"Actually, I can't, because the time stamps are recorded in-house and the data cached—" she stopped. "No one would care."

"Exactly. No one would listen to that. Though you and I know the truth, the truth is harder to explain. Hard to comprehend. Their version is easier, makes more sense, superficially."

Riley ran it through her mind. "Sommers has it tied up into a neat little narrative that is simply made for soundbites. Henry Yu was a sleeper agent for the Chinese. When he saw an incriminating video come in from one of our satellites, he doctored the video. He had the skills for it and the opportunity. He called in his young lover—me—to help him do it, then blew his brains out in remorse. Or I blew his brains out, take your pick. Either way, I am complicit."

Riley breathed out her stress, her hand on Pierce's. He turned his hand and laced it with hers and it grounded her. His hand was warm and strong. He was warm and strong. His company was behind her, Jacob Black's company was behind her. Her besties, the Queens of IT, were behind her. She wasn't alone, she had smart strong people behind her.

She felt rage rising up. Riley rarely felt angry. Putting her mother to bed high, seeing her father drive away without looking back, knowing she'd never see him again—those things hadn't made her mad, they'd made her sad.

The Boss from Hell at NSA had made her want to retreat from the world. Getting mad would have gained her nothing. All four of them—Felicity, Hope, Emma, Riley—had realized that the only thing they could do was quit, because he held all the power.

So anger wasn't really a big part of her life.

But now? Now, every cell in her body was suffused with rage, red-hot and pulsing. She knew, academically, that there were bad people in the world. All you had to do was open the newspapers and voilà. There they were. But now there were people willing to *risk war* for their own personal gain. Or to advance in a career. Or not to lose face. God only knew what kinds of justifications they were finding. Quite willing to tear up her life just for telling the truth, and not at all afraid of ruining millions, maybe billions, of lives in a war.

War was slippery. She was sure there were people planning on a 'splendid little war.' One that would test new weaponry, make some people a lot of money, shake things up. But war could escape their grasp and grow. Become World War III. End civilization. And they didn't care.

It made her a little crazy with rage, and that is when the idea came to her.

She looked at Pierce, sober and attentive. Willing—more than willing—to protect her with his life. Then she looked at Jacob Black on the screen, undoubtedly one of the good guys. He was working hard to stop this, for no reason other than it was the right thing to do.

"Guys," she said, and both sharpened their attention. "Let's fight back."

14

"No!" Pierce jumped up, the office chair skittering away. He thrust his hands in his hair, eyes wild. "Absolutely not! Don't even think about it! This is crazy! Black, you talk some sense into her."

On the screen, Jacob Black looked thoughtful.

"Black!" Pierce raised his voice, which Riley thought not too many people did to Jacob Black. Black didn't look mad, though. Just pensive. "What the fucking *hell!*"

Riley side-eyed Pierce, then turned to Jacob Black. "They're not going to stop, are they? Not just trying to get to me, but they're not going to stop the march to war. Cooler heads might prevail in the end, but real damage will be done. And in any case, my life will be ruined."

Black inclined his head. "That's right."

"So my plan, if it works, can potentially stop both things from happening, right?"

He waited a beat. "Yes."

Pierce crackled with energy. She was surprised lightning bolts weren't shooting out of his fingertips. "If! If the plan works! It's got a million moving parts and you're counting on Adrian

Sommers being able to open his mouth without telling a lie. Not to mention the danger to Riley."

Riley put her hand on his forearm and could feel the electricity. He was of course right. It was a crazy plan, but it was the only one they had. On another screen, Hope and Emma were watching her without saying anything. They'd listened carefully as she explained the plan to Black and Pierce. They hadn't said anything at all, because Pierce was taking up all the oxygen.

For all Riley knew, they thought she was crazy, too.

She drew in a deep, calming breath. "Pierce. Let's break it down, pretend it's an IT problem. I imagine you do the same when planning a mission. You first break it down into all its parts. So will you let me do that? Explain the plan step by step?"

Pierce opened his mouth and Black stepped in. "Jordan." Black's voice had dropped about seven octaves and it had massive amounts of command in it. Riley had no idea what you had to do to get a voice like that, but it worked. Pierce's mouth shut with an audible click.

"Sit. Down." Black said, the voice of God, and Pierce sat as if his legs had gone out from under him.

But Riley stood, because she liked delivering briefs on her feet. "Okay, I think we all agree that the situation is devolving fast. There are a lot of actors involved, including the military of two super powers, but it all began with one man, Adrian Sommers. I did some digging, and though Sommers is CEO of the Sommers Group, a security firm, it is nothing like ASI or Black Inc." She ignored what sounded like a growl from Black. "I did a deep dive into the Sommers Group's activities and did my best to get a handle on Sommers' personality." She wrinkled her nose. "It wasn't pleasant. Sommers seems to be a money-obsessed man with no scruples. There are a lot of those around. So money is a weak spot. And another thing. What struck me, digging through his emails, is the degree to which he is susceptible to flattery. And also how fragile his ego is, which is odd for the owner of a security company. You guys aren't known for your thin skin and sensibilities."

She slanted a glance at Pierce and looked straight at Black in the monitor. He sketched the tiniest of smiles.

"Instead, Adrian Sommers can blow up at the slightest sign of what he considers disrespect, but can be calmed down with flattery. The more ornate the better. So that's another element."

"I don't see how—" Pierce began hotly, but Riley lifted her index finger. She had to get all her reasoning out all at once. Because Pierce was spoiling for a fight.

"So the first thing about a trap is to set it and entice the trapee to come. And my instinct tells me that I need to play to his ego. Contact him. Tell him how smart he's been. How scared I am. I am completely in his hands. I have this weapon which isn't working but which can still trip him up. I don't want it. I wandered into this whole situation by chance, by mistake. I'm just an admin drone who happened on some info and my life got derailed. I want my life back and I'm scared. I'll give him anything he wants."

Jacob Black tilted his head. "You're going to have to record what he says. But he's going to frisk you for recording equipment. He will have a detector and will find it no matter where it is. And he might insist on being out in the open so what you say can't be recorded from a distance."

Riley didn't answer immediately. She pivoted to the monitor where her friends in Portland were. "Hope, you remember Ranesh?"

"Sure." She smiled. Ranesh had been a gangly Indian kid who went through MIT with them. Sweet, goofy, and an off-the-charts genius.

"He perfected his Antz."

Hope's eyes widened. "Oh my God! That's the answer! And

good for Ranesh! He'll be a billionaire inside a decade, maybe less. Couldn't happen to a nicer guy."

Ranesh had been born a 'Dalit', an untouchable, in India. His stories of his childhood would break your heart.

Riley could feel the intense focus of Pierce and Jacob Black.

"So here's the deal. Antz are tiny drones, the size of ants or flies. They are essentially invisible and completely silent. They have powerful cameras and microphones and swarm. There's a program that puts together the film and sound into a coherent and very sharp recording. Sommers would never see them, when I get him to confess. And he'll want to confess. To show the little woman how very smart he is."

She'd seen it over and over again, a man who needed to lord it over her, prove he was smarter. Even when he wasn't. *Especially* when he wasn't. She'd seen it, Felicity had seen it, both Hope and Emma had seen it. To a certain kind of mind, lording it over her was irresistible. All four of them had looks that a man like Sommers, and men like him, inevitably underestimated. The guys at ASI and Jacob Black were not among those men.

"You don't understand, Riley." Pierce was so stressed the cords in his neck stood out. He was trying really hard to look and sound reasonable, but his hands were tightly fisted and his jaws bunched as if he were chewing the words. "This is a man who was trained by the US government to be a killer but didn't absorb at all the notion of rules of engagement. You know I had a commander like that, and he was a stone-cold killer. Adrian Sommers wouldn't think twice about snuffing you out. He'd probably like that. There has got to be another way. I can't have you stake yourself out like a goat for the monster to swallow."

"Well, I can give him an incentive to keep me alive. And as for trying to kill me, what do I have you guys for? Decoration?"

He huffed out a breath like a bull. "He'll send operators who'll target you."

Riley laid a hand along his jaw, this man who was finding it hard to contain his horror at the idea of her getting hurt, killed. The skin under her palm was hot, as if he had a fever.

"I'm counting on that," she said softly. "You guys will have full body suits of very thin graphene which will make you impermeable to infrared, and has some stealth-cloaking ability. You won't be invisible but close to it. We will have drones and you'll see all his men and you guys will take them off the board, one by one. You'll be listening to everything we say and you'll have time to react.

"No one can react faster than a goddamn bullet," Pierce said heatedly.

"But—" she began.

"Jordan." Jacob Black had put on his Voice of God again. "No one wants to see Riley go in harm's way. No one, especially you, I understand that, and not me, either. But … I don't see that we have any choice. Sommers is not going to stop. He has eighty-five operators, and he can keep them going nonstop to find Riley and eliminate her for as long as it takes. We'd have to protect her 24/7/365, nonstop, and all we have to do is make one mistake and it's over. Riley is right in wanting to take proactive steps to get this over with, and to possibly stop a shooting war. There's that."

"That's easy enough for you to say!" Pierce shouted the words. "She means fuckall to you and she means everything to me!"

There was a shocked silence, but Pierce didn't apologize. The only sound was his heavy breathing.

"Pierce." Riley ran her hand along his arm, touched. She was putting herself in harm's way and she was scared, too. But along-side the fear was her desire to *live*. To live freely and not in hiding. To live and see where this … this *thing* she had going with Pierce would lead them. "It's okay," she said softly.

"It's not okay." Pierce leaned forward on two fists, his face close to the monitor's camera. "Send me," he urged Black. "Let me go and make whatever arrangements Riley was going to make. She doesn't have to do this. She's not trained if it all goes to shit. I am. Send *me*."

Oh Pierce, she thought. Touched beyond words. She blinked back tears.

"It's precisely because you are trained that he wouldn't let you get within a thousand feet of him," she said softly. "He'd never see you as defenseless. Someone he can brag to because he's won. He'd be rightly scared of you and he'd come at you with everything he's got. And we'd never get a confession out of him. A confession at this point is the only thing that can stop this relentless march. A confession is the only thing that can save my life. A life worth living, that is."

He whirled, grabbed both her hands with his. "I can't let you do it," he said, his voice stark. "I can't lose you just when I've found you. I love you."

Tears shimmered in her eyes. It was the very first time in her life someone said that to her, and it had to be in the middle of danger and possible warfare.

"Hey!" Hope's voice sounded panicked. "Check in with Online News. Right now!"

Riley switched to ON and listened in horror.

An Asian woman was on screen. *Chinese attack imminent* read the chyron along the bottom of the screen.

"This is Jessica Chan, live from Singapore. The Chinese People's Liberation Army has sent 80 warplanes, including fighter jets, reconnaissance craft and refuellers, into Taiwan's Air Defence Identification Zone, according to the Pentagon's spokeswoman. The spokeswoman also said that 42 planes had crossed the median line—the de facto border in the Taiwan strait between Taiwan and China. The USS George H.W. Bush has sent up twelve F-16 fighter jets, each equipped with six AIM-9X Sidewinder missiles. A spokesman for the Pentagon

issued this declaration. "The US is dedicated to the defense of Taiwan and will vigorously respond to any aggression from the People's Republic of China." The reporter put down a sheet of paper and stared directly into the camera. *"Our sources say that plans for a war with China are being discussed at the highest levels in the Pentagon. That's all for now."*

Riley's heart hammered in horror. Everything was slipping out of control, sliding down into the hell of a war, a war that could escalate and plunge the world into flames.

Whatever she could do to stop it, she had to. And fast.

She picked up the phone.

15

Pierce could only listen and watch as Riley did her thing.

"Yes, yes, tell him I'll wait."

Riley had had the Queens route the call to the Sommers Group through an anonymizer and had put the call on speaker phone. Her voice was dull, low. Defeated even. But she was standing straight as an arrow and her eyes were flashing with anger and determination.

She'd been bounced from secretary to admin to vice president, always saying the same thing. That she wanted to speak to Adrian Sommers. And that she was Riley Robinson and he'd want to speak to her.

Finally, a deep voice. "This is Sommers. Who is this?" Impatient. *I'm a busy man. Don't waste my time.*

Riley made her own voice soft, barely audible. "Mr. Sommers, this is Riley Robinson."

"Who?"

Riley rolled her eyes, but you couldn't hear anything but defeat and desperation in her voice.

"Riley Robinson. Sir."

"Don't know anyone by that name." His voice was dismissive, abrupt.

"Wait!"

"Yes?"

"I think you do know my name. Sir." She drew in a deep, audible breath as if steeling herself to something. "I caught the original of the tape of your men in

Congo."

Silence.

"I reported it to Henry Yu."

"Don't know what you're talking about, but I'll hear you out."

Riley started to speak then gave a great sob. Tears were in her voice, but not in her eyes. "I want my life back! Please! Oh please! It's been hell since I intercepted the satellite download. It was pure coincidence I caught it and my life has been hell ever since! Oh God, please help me!"

Pierce was amazed. If you just listened to the voice, you got the impression of a helpless young woman, in over her head, trying desperately to disentangle herself from a situation bigger than she was. He almost believed her story that the video had fallen into her lap by coincidence, rather than her pursuing the story.

As long as he wasn't looking at her, because she looked like a warrior. Eyes flashing, face set, body arrow-straight.

After another moment's silence, Sommers spoke. "I don't know what this has to do with me."

A shudder ran through her. It was as if Riley's light blue eyes shot lightning bolts, streaks of energy it almost hurt to watch.

He stood, ready to fight, to shoot, to do whatever the fuck she needed, but she didn't need him. This was a situation he couldn't help her with, in any way.

He would have gladly shot Sommers, if he could have. But he couldn't. And he didn't even know whether eliminating

Sommers from the face of the earth, as satisfying as that sounded, would make Riley safe. There were others involved in this shitshow in the Sommers Group, and probably in the Pentagon.

All he could do was stand with her, ready to help in any way he could. And he knew ASI and Black Inc. stood ready, too.

But for the moment, it was her show.

"I-I think you do, Mr. Sommers." Man, Riley deserved an Oscar. It was pitch-perfect. Timid and frightened, but sure of her facts, and determined. Exactly as would be a computer nerd who found herself in deep waters and wanted out. Sommers couldn't know his web had snared a snarling dragon, not a timid girl. "I think you know what I have and what I can testify to. But ... I don't want it! I want out!" Her voice rose almost to hysteria. "I don't want any part of this! Let me give you everything I have and just ... just *leave me alone!*"

Pierce was standing right beside her and was almost convinced himself that she was harmless. All she wanted was out.

But he was standing right beside her, and all he could see was her determination. She wasn't timid and afraid. She was brave and super *super* pissed.

Out of the receiver came a humming sound, someone contemplating. "Well, Ms. ... Robinson, is it?" As if he didn't have a complete dossier on her right in front of him. "I still don't know what you want, but I am willing to talk."

"Oh, thank God!" It was as if the exclamation came from deep within her. The answer to her prayers. "Yes! Oh my God, all I want is my life back and to put this whole mess behind me!"

"Well, let's see what kind of mess there is then, Ms. Robinson." Sommers' tone had turned avuncular. Powerful older man going out of his way to help young woman. Out of the goodness of his heart. Pierce's teeth ground together. This man had tried several times to kill Riley. "We should meet."

"Yes! Yes!" Riley sobbed. "And I know just the place! Rock Creek Park. Out in the open. Safer for everyone."

"No, Ms. Robinson, I think it's best that you come to me—"

"No no!" Here her voice turned fearful. "I want it to be a public place. Picnic Grove 11, just off Nebraska Avenue. Along Binam Drive. I run there several times a week. I need a place that feels familiar."

There was a pause. Pierce was certain Sommers was checking it out, and he was too. Picnic Grove 11 in Rock Creek Park was a picnic table with a stone grill to one side, with a small creek running behind it. Groves surrounded it, but about fifty yards away.

"I'll meet you there in half an hour," she said hurriedly. "I'll bring everything. I want all of this to be *over.*" And she closed the connection, opened the burner phone, took out the battery and crushed it beneath her heel.

A blur of her fingers on her laptop and a man's face appeared. He looked Indian, or at least Southeast Asian. Clearly a nerd, with a half-assed mangy goatee, glasses slipping down his nose, huge brown eyes.

He wore a serious expression.

"Ranesh, good to see you. I don't have much time."

"Got it. Hope explained the situation. I'll rendezvous with your guys and bring the Antz and the controller. Make sure I have their GPS coordinates. We'll nail this guy!"

"Thanks Ranesh. Pierce Jordan will be giving you the coordinates. You'll rendezvous with Pierce and Jacob Black and his men."

Silence. "Jacob Black? *The* Jacob Black?"

"Yeah. He doesn't bite."

Riley blacked out the monitor and muted the sound. "Hear

that, Jacob?" she said without turning around. "You will *not* bite my friend. He's sensitive."

"Promise," Black growled.

She turned everything back on. "Okay, Ranesh. I'm counting on you. I don't think it's an exaggeration to say that you will be saving my life."

"Count on me, Riley." The voice shook but sounded determined.

Riley turned around, hugged Pierce tightly. She felt taut as a wire.

"Pierce, Jacob, send drones, the quiet kind, over the area and find Sommers' men and take them off the board. Quietly. And not permanently. Have Emma guide the drones, she's the best we've got."

Pierce remembered Raul saying that Emma's mastery of drones saved the day, and saved their bacon back in San Francisco. He said she was the best he'd ever seen.

"Right."

"And you all will be swathed in the new graphene suits. You have them don't you, Jacob?" She put her face in front of the monitor camera and saw Black nod.

She addressed both of them. "Emma will neutralize any drones that aren't ours. She'll put their recordings on a loop. Behind the picnic table, about 50 or 60 yards from the creek, is the densest bush. If you can stage there, you should be okay. I'll make sure Sommers is facing the bushes. Ranesh will be directing the Antz. Put what we're saying and the video images directly online. On YouTube and Instagram. Have Hope piggyback on to a big TV network, live. Several networks, if she can. I don't think anyone can cry *deepfake* on something that is happening live, though they will try. God, with any luck we can stop everything in its tracks. We'll need snipers with a laser pointer in the bushes across the creek, able to send a laser beam to Sommers's heart where he can see it."

She was rattling off commands, and ordinarily Pierce would have bristled at commands from a civilian, and he knew Black would resent it, too, except the commands were sound. They had to trust her.

"Okay, off with you. Pierce, either steal another car, or have one of Jacob's men pick you up. I'm Ubering."

"What?" Pierce shot a glance at the monitor where Black looked as dumbfounded as he did.

"I might beat him to the place, but you can be sure he'll be checking cameras. I need to have him see me as weak and defeated. Arriving in an Uber will just show how alone I am." She lifted her hands, turned around. Unzipped the hoodie, showed the tight tank top. Lifted her ankles, the tight yoga style pants hid nothing besides her lovely legs. "He'll make me show that I don't have any recording equipment. I'll just have my fanny pack with some cash in it, and a thumb drive, and that's it. The thumb drive will have the original video of his soldiers and that's it. I'll convince him that I only have one copy that is in a safe deposit box, and if I am convinced he'll let me be, I'll send the message to self-destruct."

"He's perfectly capable of torturing you for it," Black said evenly.

"Yes, but he would have to take me prisoner first. And what are you guys there for? To look pretty?"

No, Pierce and Black weren't going to be there for decoration, they would be there armed and ready to blow Sommers' head off, if necessary. Pierce really wanted that, but knew it would be much better to have Sommers unmasked and humiliated, his life ruined, and this whole fucking mess with China resolved.

But he also really, *really* wanted to blow Sommers' head off. He'd nearly had Riley killed.

Riley was almost hopping with nerves. "Oh God, oh God," she chanted. "Let it all go well."

Yeah, they all hoped it would go well. A lot was hanging on the next couple of hours. Maybe even the fate of the world.

Her phone chimed and she looked at it. "Uber's here. Gotta go!"

And she ran, slamming the door behind her.

RILEY WAS AGITATED on the ride to Rock Creek Park. That was fine. She was *supposed* to look nervous. Nervous and timid and scared. Easily intimidated. Manipulable. She was nervous, it was true, but also enraged, so she had to operate on two levels. Looking scared and hiding her rage.

She was also really scared, too. The plan to unmask Sommers had been created on the fly, with a thousand moving parts. It depended on Pierce and Jacob working well with the nerdiest nerd on the face of the earth, Ranesh. Who didn't react well to being dominated, having been bullied as a child. But she trusted them to figure Ranesh out and treat him with kid gloves.

Everything also depended on the Antz, which were being field-tested for the first time right now.

Ranesh was a genius, but beta trials were necessary for a reason. The Antz had never been used before. They could be a flop and this whole thing could end in a bloodbath.

She had no comms. There was no way Sommers wouldn't figure out if she was able to communicate with her team. But her team would be able to hear her, thanks to Ranesh. It could come down to split-second timing. She could end up with nothing but a fistful of ashes and the world burning down. Or she could end up with a bullet in the head.

Don't think that way, she chided herself.

This had to work, had to.

On the way over, a news site had said that China was testing a hypersonic missile glide system that could evade US missile defense systems.

She refused to be even a minor part of a war starting up, not when she suddenly had so much to live for.

She was in mortal danger, speeding her way to a clever and evil man whom she had to outwit, and who had already tried to kill her.

But watching over her would be the handsomest, coolest man she'd ever seen. Not to mention the most fascinating and kindest man she'd ever met and who somehow, by some magical alchemy that only happened in novels and role-playing games, seemed as interested in her as she was in him. And who was also a god in bed. A man who had redefined sex for her.

A man who'd said he loved her.

A man who was willing to lay his life on the line for her.

A man in a million, someone she couldn't have dreamt up in her most heated dreams because she didn't know someone like him existed.

The world had shifted on its axis. Where the future had been this vaguely interesting place that might yield up new software, a nice restaurant, a good movie—now the future was this incredibly magical place where every single moment could lead to blinding pleasure. Where sitting on a sofa holding hands flooded her with endorphins. Where waking up with Pierce by her side was this amazing experience because who knew what the day would bring?

She didn't want to lose that, not just as she'd found it.

She'd never had love in her life. And now that she had it, it was on the cusp of extreme danger. She couldn't lose this.

She psyched herself up as the Uber driver drove along Nebraska, took a little turnoff on Oregon and there it was. The path into Rock Creek Park she often took when running. She knew the place intimately, which was why she chose it. She would be in the weeds here, dealing with a man she'd never met and who was vicious and calculating and powerful. To her advantage, she was familiar with the place, and above all, she had really good guys on her side. Not only good guys, but guys who knew what they were doing.

Plus the Antz, making their test run today, right now. Guided by Ranesh, the smartest man she'd ever met. And who was a good friend.

She paid the Uber and walked slowly toward the entrance, then onto the hiking trail. The picnic table was a little farther in —you had to go over a small hillock. Ah, there it was.

It wasn't much to look at. The table was weathered and cracked; the barbecue area was run-down. The last people to use it hadn't cleaned up, so it was full of charcoal.

She looked around carefully. If her guys had set up, she couldn't see them. They'd have driven much more quickly than the Uber guy, so they should be here. If they were, they were invisible.

Her vision clouded a little, like gauze had been placed over a part of the scene, then it cleared up. It took her a moment to realize what it was.

The Antz!! Ranesh had set up and had sent his Antz over to her. It was brilliant. She couldn't see any of them individually just a tiny hint of cloud where they swarmed. There they were on the tabletop, almost completely invisible. The tabletop of the picnic table was in bad shape with crevices and flaking wood. The Antz couldn't be seen. She bent down. Under the tabletop were lots of Antz, barely visible, presumably the voice recording ones.

There was still no one around, so she said, "Can you hear me?"

A small, frail brown hand shot up from the bushes and she smiled.

"Ranesh, are you okay?" Two hands shot up, thumbs up.

She would never have known Ranesh was there. She trusted that Pierce and Jacob Black and his men were stationed at strategic places, even if she couldn't see them. They were good.

Well, of course.

She also trusted them to deal with Sommers' men.

Otherwise she was in deepest shit, because Sommers was definitely one of the bad guys, and the men in his employ were, too. They had killed Henry Yu and had come after her twice.

Adrian Sommers was a treacherous man. *Remember that, Riley.*

And there he was, striding down the path as if he owned it.

Riley watched him approaching. She'd seen photos and had seen the photo in his company's brochure. That photo had been heavily photoshopped, dropping pounds and wrinkles. But even with the pounds and wrinkles back on, he was a handsome man if you squinted. Tall, powerfully built, with even features. He spent a lot of money on himself. That haircut was a $300 one, at least. He was wearing a couple thousand dollars in linen shirt, light cashmere sweater and linen trousers. And another thousand on beautiful boots. No man-jewelry, though. He was in the security business, so jewelry would probably be frowned on.

Sommers stopped about ten feet from the table and she nearly had a heart attack. Had he seen someone? Could he see the Antz?

"Stand up," he said, cold command in his voice. The avuncular good guy was gone and he was playing hardball. "Come around."

"Okay." She stood up, stood away from the table.

"Show me you aren't wearing a wire."

She put on an astonished look. "A what?"

"A wire, goddammit." When she blinked, still looking baffled, he added, "Recording equipment."

Riley reared back. "Oh! Of course. Sorry."

She'd chosen her wardrobe well. Sports bra, tank top, zip-up. Tight stretch pants. She took off the zip-up, lifted up the tank top, turned around in a full circle. Lifted one leg then the other, pulling the pant leg bottom up to her knees then letting them fall back. Not even the most paranoid person in the world could imagine she had equipment on her.

Near the table she saw the faintest hint of a shimmer. No, she'd outsourced all of that.

"Any pockets?"

"On the zip-up."

"Turn them inside out."

Obediently, Riley turned the pockets inside out.

"The-the thing there." He waved a finger at the tabletop. "The mini purse thing."

"The fanny pack?"

"Yeah." His voice turned sarcastic. "The fanny pack."

It was small. She picked it up, unzipped the top and turned it upside down. Three twenty-dollar bills and a flash drive. Sommers' attention was riveted on the flash drive. She scooped up the money and flash drive and pushed everything back into the fanny pack.

Not until I get what I want. It couldn't have been clearer if she had spoken the words aloud.

He gestured with his hand for her to sit down, an almost old-fashioned gesture, as if they were in a drawing room and he were inviting her to tea and not to a fight to the death.

She sat down, aware that they were being livestreamed. The Antz would be concentrated on her face and on his, but the livestream would only be showing Sommers. Her voice would be altered, but not his.

Behind her would be Pierce and Black and Ranesh, and maybe one or two of Black's men. Other operators would be behind Sommers.

She sat off-center to him, pretending there were splinters in the bench right across from him. If someone had to shoot him from the front, she didn't want to be in the way, and if someone had to shoot from the back, she didn't want the bullet to go through him and hit her.

It had been made clear to her that the guns they would be using would be high-powered rifles.

From now on, it was a deathly game.

She had to guide the conversation, so she started. "Listen, Mr. Sommers—"

"*Colonel* Sommers, to you," he interjected.

"Colonel Sommers," she repeated obediently. Body language abject, head slightly bowed, hands clasped in front of her, trembling. "I'm here to tell you—ask you—let me go. I want out. I'm nobody. I'm an office drone in the NSO who just happened upon a satellite video a couple of days ago. It was pure chance I caught it. My brief is the Chinese, and the Chinese are very active in Congo." She looked up suddenly and could barely contain the contempt she felt. "It wasn't Chinese soldiers in that initial video I saw. It was American soldiers, wearing the Sommers Group uniform, slaughtering American scientists from the CDC studying a new strain of Ebola."

"That's slander," he said evenly. "I could sue you."

Riley sighed. They were easing into it. "No, you can't and you won't. Because I can prove in a court of law that my video is the original, which was later turned into a deepfake. There might be a moment in the future when deepfakes cannot be distinguished from reality but we're not there yet. The court of public opinion might be fooled, but a court of law won't be. You're not going to sue me."

He smiled, lips stretching wide, the affable businessman completely gone. It was a smile of utter cruelty. Of the apex predator crushing his prey.

He held up his phone, slid his finger across and a video appeared. Please God the Antz were picking it up.

"What am I seeing?" She frowned, moved closer. It was dark-ish. Two people meeting in a park. A man and a woman. The video zeroed in on the face of the man and she gasped. Rudy Fillmore. The notorious traitor, who'd sold classified documents to anyone who'd buy them and had filled the airwaves for months. There were two documentaries and a Netflix series made about him.

The camera shifted and she gasped again. It was her! She was handing over documents to the infamous Rudy Fillmore. Unmistakably her, blonde hair bright in the light of a street lamp. She was dressed for running, like she was now. She turned and the likeness was perfect. It was uncanny. Even she would testify that it was her, though it wasn't and she'd never seen Rudy Fillmore in person.

"That's a fake," she said, frowning.

"A good one. A very good one. And this will be sent to every news agency, every political blog, every news program. It'll be Riley Robinson Traitor, 24/7 for weeks."

She squinted. Rudy Fillmore had disappeared from the face of the earth six months ago, and reappeared in Moscow a week later, claiming asylum.

"What's the date of this?"

Sommers turned the cell around and squinted. "January 6th of this year."

"I was at a conference in Cancun on January 6th. It won't stand up in court."

"Maybe not, but by the time you start defending yourself, your name will be trashed, you'll be a famous traitor, and no one will believe you. That's what will happen if you talk about this story."

"About you deepfaking the video? I imagine you asked our section head, Morris Sartan, to do it. When I told Henry Yu, he said he'd take it to his boss, Morris Sartan. Morris would have the skills, you certainly wouldn't."

He smirked. "I don't need those skills. I have other ones."

Tears trembled on her eyelashes. They were real. "You didn't have to kill Henry. He was just a messenger."

"He had to go, and so did you. But if you keep your mouth shut and disappear, I can let this thing go. It's become bigger than us, anyway."

A tear fell. Her voice shook. "You might be causing a *war*," she whispered. "To protect your reputation."

He shrugged, and she could see that for him, the meeting was over. He'd secured her silence. If she talked, he'd destroy her. She had to hand over the thumb drive.

It had been a successful meeting and he'd come out on top.

Riley raised her voice. "Did you guys get all that? Are we done?"

And a deep voice rose from a thousand tiny drones, surprisingly clear. Jacob Black. "Oh yeah, we got what we needed. Sommers you fuckhead, you're going away forever."

Sommers' face froze with shock, then turned deep red. He reached out with one meaty hand to grab her wrist and the other reached to his lower back.

"Don't even think of it, Sommers," Black's deep disembodied voice said.

"Look down," Riley suggested.

Sommers looked down and saw four laser beams centered on his heart so precisely they converged, rock steady, almost in a circle.

"Behind those guns are Navy SEALs, Sommers," she said.

"Make a move and you're dead. I can absolutely assure you that they are itching to pull the trigger."

"Better believe it," Black said, voice deep and resonant and clear. "One twitch and you're gone to whatever hell awaits a traitor and a man who'd start a world war. We'd be really happy to blow you to that hell, right men?"

Three men growled as Sommers quivered with rage. "You!" he shouted to Riley. "You bitch! You've been nothing but trouble. You'll regret this, I'll see you—"

But she wasn't listening. She was running back to the thick copse of trees and Pierce was running toward her, across the little creek with ankle-deep water, catching her up in his arms so tightly she couldn't breathe. It didn't make any difference because he was kissing her and she was breathing through him.

Pierce broke the kiss, tilted his head back and Riley was astonished to see tears in his eyes. Big bad warrior, crying?

"Are you crying?"

"No," he sniffed, wiping his eyes. "Yes. Goddammit, I nearly watched the woman I love killed. I have a right."

He pulled back and stared her in the face, expectantly.

"What?"

"Say it."

She was crying for real, not trying to hide it, tears streaming down her face. "All right." She laughed. "I love you. I thought I wasn't going to see you again."

"You're never doing anything like that, ever again." His voice was low, fervent. "Ever, *ever* again."

"No." Her voice was just as fervent. "Climbing walls at the gym will be the most dangerous thing I ever do. Ever. I—"

Her eyes widened. She'd forgotten. How could she have forgotten? "Ranesh!" she cried. "Is he okay? Is he hurt?" Ranesh was a gentle soul and she'd thrown him in the middle of danger. Oh God, if anything had happened to him, she'd never forgive herself! Even if he wasn't hurt, surely he'd be traumatized for life.

Pierce laughed. "He's fine. See for yourself. Ranesh! Come out!"

The bushes crackled and shook and Ranesh emerged, followed by Jacob Black. Ranesh was smiling, hair standing up on end.

"Riley!" he shouted.

"Ranesh! Are you okay?"

She ran to him, held him by his scrawny upper arms, examining him from head to toe. He was beaming and he looked like he'd grown a couple of inches in the last half hour.

He was bouncing from foot to foot, hopped up on excitement.

"That was *awesome!* And my Antz performed brilliantly, didn't they, Jacob?"

He looked back and up and up at Jacob Black's face, clearly overwhelmed with hero worship. Jacob?

Jacob put a hand on Ranesh's shoulder, covering it entirely. "Absolutely. They are amazing. You are amazing! We're going to work together, make millions of dollars. The Antz are a real game changer."

"We'll go on another adventure?" Ranesh looked happy and about five years old.

"Oh yeah. Count on it." Jacob Black smiled. It looked really weird on his austere face. Riley was surprised his face didn't crack. "We'll go on lots of adventures."

They walked over to the picnic table. Two of Black's men had put zip ties on Sommers, who was uselessly resisting, shouting incomprehensibly. No one paid him any attention.

"Where are his men?" Riley asked.

Pierce smiled. "Taken care of. Don't worry about them. Now."

His expression changed, turned serious. He braced his legs apart as if expecting a hurricane. "You and I have things to discuss."

Riley put her hands on his chest. To reassure herself that he was okay. And because it felt amazing. "Yes?"

"Black wants you to come work with him. He has offices all over the States and could probably offer you a ton of money. But I want you to come back to Portland with me. Work with ASI. They'll give you lots of money, too. Not as much as Black, but you'd be working with Felicity, Hope and Emma. And me."

He braced even more. "I won't take *no* for an answer."

And waited.

Well, she thought, *let's see.* Go to work for a huge corporation where she knew no one, in some city where she knew no one. That was how she'd started at the NSO and she still didn't have any friends.

Orrrr ... move to Portland, Oregon, which everyone said was a charming little city. Work with her best friends, who were really happy there. Work with Pierce who was the love of her life.

Yes or no?

No question.

"Yes," she said. "Oh, yes."

EPILOGUE

THREE MONTHS LATER, THE GRANGE, PORTLAND, OREGON

"Watch it, Pierce!" Metal's anxious voice rang out. "Don't drop him!"

Pierce was a sharpshooter and combat driver with incredibly steady hands and was as strong as an ox. He wasn't about to drop a three-month-old baby, so he ignored Metal. As was everyone else, as Metal anxiously made the rounds, following his amazingly cute twin boys, bouncing from lap to lap.

There were lots of laps. It was Raul and Emma's engagement party, and the huge place in the foothills of Mt. Hood was full. A lot of them were Raul's extended family, come from all over to meet Emma. She charmed them all, speaking excellent Spanish and helping the younger members with their videogame scores.

That they were all together celebrating two people in love was a miracle, considering that there had been a very real possibility that the world would be burned to ashes in a nuclear war.

When Riley's video, pieced together brilliantly by Antz software, hit the airwaves, it didn't make that much of a splash with the general public, but it made a big splash at the Pentagon, where the Sommers Group had been about to be awarded contracts worth over a billion dollars.

Lots of red faces. Lots of careers unmade. And lots of careers made of people who'd pleaded for reason to prevail. And reason prevailed. The aggressive moves immediately ceased, and there was talk of new trade deals and a treaty. Everyone walking back gingerly from the threshold of war.

Adrian Sommers' trial was scheduled to begin in a month.

Riley had been working for ASI for two months and had loved every single second of it. It was a great place to work and she was working with her best friends in the whole world. She slotted in easily, and the Queens of IT were grateful for her help, since Felicity had given birth and had been on maternity leave, though working from home. The company had experienced one of its regular expansions of business, and by the time Felicity came back, they were all working flat-out.

Riley was incredibly happy there. The work was interesting, the bosses generous and appreciative, the ASI guys affectionate and fun.

The workplace was gorgeous, too, which didn't hurt. That was thanks to the wife of one of the Big Bosses, Suzanne Huntington, who had a magic touch with spaces. She'd designed the beautiful Grange, too, where they were celebrating the engagement, eating incredible food prepared by the wife of an ASI operator, Isabel Delvaux-Harris, a world-renowned food expert.

But the big advantage was working with Pierce, seeing Pierce almost every day. He had to travel some, all the ASI operators did, but there was an unspoken rule that if an operator was away, his wife or his woman was looked after. Pierce had had to take business trips to Boston and Mexico City and she had had to beat away the invitations to dinner with a stick.

She didn't turn down the invitations to go shopping with Suzanne and Isabel and Lauren Jackman, though. She discovered she loved shopping. Who knew?

"He's such a cutie," Pierce cooed, holding one of the twins up above his head. They were Michael and Richard—Mick and Rick—but nobody could tell them apart except for their parents. They looked a lot like Metal, but somewhere in there were Felicity's fine features.

Riley could tell that they'd be heartbreakers when they grew up.

Felicity had had the world's worst pregnancy—projectile vomiting on a regular basis—but the delivery had been straightforward and she'd been champing at the bit to come back to work almost immediately. She'd been working from home since day three after birth, though everyone told her to rest.

A whole village worth of people was looking after her babies, so she was in a corner talking to Hope and Suzanne, leaving all the anxiety to Metal.

Pierce pumped the baby—either Rick or Mick—up and down like a weight lifter pumps iron, and the baby gurgled happily, giving Pierce the most charming toothless gummy grin. Pierce grinned back.

"Who do I have here?" he asked Metal, who was watching his son bounce up and down, hands ready to catch him when Pierce dropped him.

"Mick," Metal said, though Riley couldn't see how he could tell.

"Up you go, Mick." Pierce threw him a little, catching him. Mick squealed and gurgled, tiny limbs churning. Clearly having a great time.

Then Mick farted, and he delivered an industrial level of poop, an amount so vast it overran his diapers and onesie, and ran down his little legs.

Pierce's look of horror and dismay was so funny Riley broke out in peals of laughter. As did everyone else, after an initial period of utter silence. The laughter went out in concentric circles as everyone stopped what they were doing and turned to look.

Metal grabbed his kid and went off to change his diaper, grinning. Felicity said Metal had become a champion diaper-changer. There were two kids so someone always needed a diaper changed.

A Martinez woman—either Raul's sister or a cousin or a sister-in-law, there were so many it was hard to keep them straight—had a tea towel and a bottle of water, and washed Pierce's arm right then and there.

Riley bit her lips to stop laughing and walked up to Pierce.

Luckily, he'd overcome his horror and was laughing, too. "My ma always said kids are barbarians."

His best friend Raul slapped his back. "I'm sure we'll find out for ourselves soon enough, buddy," and looked meaningfully at Emma. Emma just smiled back.

All of a sudden, the music changed and someone shouted, "Jitterbug!"

Riley and Emma looked at each other and moved to the center of the huge room. Everyone moved back to give them space.

Emma had wanted to take swing dance lessons, but Raul just couldn't do it. He had two left feet. He could parachute from ten thousand feet and dive to 300 feet and he could run obstacle courses, but he couldn't dance. Just couldn't feel the beat. So Emma asked Riley if she wanted to take lessons and yeah, Riley did. Pierce definitely did not. Riley and Emma had a fabulous time at the dance lessons and had turned out to be great dance partners. Emma was a better dancer, but Riley was more athletic and they learned from each other.

Riley had become particularly good at shuffle dancing.

The music was turned up and they clasped hands, bent their knees, found their center and they were off. Feet flying, knees shaking, bouncing and hopping and bopping. Face-to-face and then side-to-side. Riley lost herself in the music, in the movements, in the beat. It was completely different from rock climbing, where you were utterly concentrated in yourself.

Here, you lost yourself in the music and in the movements of your partner, and it was like flying. Her feet moved without her thinking about it, skirt flying around her knees.

Yep, skirt. Riley had discovered dresses and she loved them. And colors. A friend in college complained that the only color she knew was beige. Well, now she had dresses in ice cream colors. Lots of them. Pretty and frothy and she loved wearing them.

Pierce loved them, too. He particularly loved taking them off her.

Speaking of Pierce, there he was, off to the side, laughing and clapping and cheering, grinning like a loon.

Emma glanced at Riley, eyebrows raised. Riley briefly indicated herself with her thumb and Emma nodded. The music was rising, rising, and Riley grabbed Emma's hands and slid through her legs, jumping up and landing exactly as the music stopped.

The great hall erupted in cheers and applause and whistles.

Pierce grabbed her and twirled her, ending in a huge kiss. She was breathing hard and her heart was pumping and the kiss just kept it pumping, the most glorious feeling in the world.

Pierce finally lifted his head and gazed down at her, deep blue eyes gleaming. "What do you say we have our own engagement party right here some day?"

Her heart pumped harder.

"Yeah."

"That's a *yes*?"

She laughed. "That's a *yes*."

"Soon?"

She nodded. "Soon."

He turned her in his arms and faced his friends. Their friends. A wall of people who loved them.

"Hey guys, we're getting married!"

It took half an hour for the noise to die down.

THE END

ALSO BY LISA MARIE RICE

Men Of Midnight Series

Midnight Man

Midnight Run

Midnight Angel

Midnight Quest

Midnight Vengeance

Midnight Promises

Midnight Secrets

Midnight Fire

Midnight Fever

Midnight Renegade

Midnight Kiss

Midnight Embrace

Midnight Caress

Midnight Shadows

Her Billionaire Series

Charade

Masquerade

Escapade

Dangerous Passions

Reckless

Hot Secrets

The Christmas Angel

Murphy's Law

Woman On The Run

Fatal Heat

A Fine Specimen

The Italian

Don't Think Twice

Port Of Paradise

ABOUT THE AUTHOR

Lisa Marie Rice is eternally 30 years old and will never age. She is tall and willowy and beautiful. Men drop at her feet like ripe pears. She has won every major book prize in the world. She is a black belt with advanced degrees in archaeology, nuclear physics, and Tibetan literature. She is a concert pianist. Did I mention her Nobel Prize?

Of course, Lisa Marie Rice is a virtual woman and exists only at the keyboard when writing romance. She disappears when the monitor winks off.

www.ingramcontent.com/pod-product-compliance
Lightning Source LLC
Chambersburg PA
CBHW020141120726

47903CB00007B/2360